A
Circle
Unbroken

A Circle Unbroken

◆━━━━●━━━━◆

SOLLACE HOTZE

❖ ❖ ❖

CLARION BOOKS
TICKNOR & FIELDS: A HOUGHTON MIFFLIN COMPANY
NEW YORK

Acknowledgments

I would like to give special thanks to the following people: my nephew, Sollace Mitchell, who first introduced me to Rachel; Jan Milella, who so generously shared her research materials; Jean Tolle who showed me where Rachel's journey should begin; Mary Shura Craig who helped me to see where the journey should end; the members of the Barrington Writers' Workshop who gave me their support and always kept me headed in the right direction.

Clarion Books
Ticknor & Fields, a Houghton Mifflin Company
Text copyright © 1988 by Sollace Hotze
All rights reserved.

For information about permission to reproduce
selections from this book, write to Permissions,
Houghton Mifflin Company, 2 Park Street,
Boston, MA 02108
Printed in the U.S.A.

Library of Congress Cataloging-in-Publication Data
Hotze, Sollace.
  A circle unbroken.
  Summary: Captured by a roving band of Sioux Indians
and brought up as the chief's daughter, Rachel is re-
captured by her white family and finds it difficult
to adjust, as she longs to return to the tribe.
  1. Dakota Indians—Juvenile fiction. [1. Dakota
Indians—Fiction. 2. Indians of North America—
Captivities—Fiction] I. Title.
PZ7.H8114Ci 1988   [Fic]   88-2569
ISBN 0-89919-733-7

P 10 9 8 7 6 5 4 3 2 1

For my father and mother—
who gave me the courage to be.

1

The wind jittered the leaves. It snatched them from the trees along the banks of the river and swirled them in gusts across the plain on that early October day in 1845. The girl the Sioux called Kata Wi, Burning Sun, stood near the tumbling stream and gazed westward across the rolling prairie toward *Paha Sapa*, the Black Hills. She listened to the nervous flutter of leaves. A sharp uneasiness cut across the midday hush, prickling the base of her scalp.

She squatted beside the Indian girl of sixteen, one winter younger than she, who knelt close beside her, dressing a buffalo skin on the bank of the swollen creek. Kata Wi pressed the palms of her hands against the ground, feeling the earth still warm against her skin. Beneath the earth, a faint tremor reverberated against her outstretched fingers.

"Tanka," she said softly. The girl whom Kata Wi called Little Sister looked up in response. "Listen, Tanka. Do you hear a strange sound?"

Tanka lifted her head, brushing the unbound black hair back from her round face with its high cheekbones that seemed to make her dark eyes sink deeper into their sockets. "I hear the wind, Kata Wi, and the water running in the river. But those aren't strange sounds." She searched the eyes of Kata Wi beside her. "What do you hear?"

"I'm not sure. I have a strange feeling."

Tanka looked at Kata Wi with concern.

"Listen," Kata Wi said again and pressed her hands more firmly against the hard earth. The faint tremors became a steady beat. "Horses," she said slowly, turning her face eastward where the Bad River traversed the rolling plains until it emptied into the great Missouri. "And riders, coming this way, following the path of the river."

"Perhaps it is the men, returning from the hunt."

"But they would be riding from the north. And it is much too soon. They left only two suns ago."

"Perhaps it is traders from the white man's fort. Or trappers going early into the mountains for the winter."

"Perhaps," Kata Wi replied and stood up. She moved slowly along the edge of the stream. Tanka was probably right. It must be either traders or trappers coming up the river from the post at Fort Tecumseh. But, although their small band from the Oglala Sioux tribe was always welcomed for trading at the post, the white hunters and traders in the area traveled in small groups, and these men usually stayed clear of the Sioux camps on the great plains.

She rounded the bend of the stream, peering ahead to discover the cause of her misgivings. Far in the distance a band of horsemen galloped toward her from the east, following the path of the river as it wound through clumps of trees. There was something furtive and secretive in their approach. Instead of cutting a straight line across the open plain, they zigzagged through the trees, moving from one grove to another, staying always within the cover of the foliage, now bright with autumn hues of crimson and gold but still thick and heavy on the branches.

These men were neither Sioux nor Indians from another tribe. The horses carried saddles and the men were fully clothed and wore broadbrimmed hats. These were white men.

As they cleared one grove and headed across the opening between the clumps of trees, she counted eight, too many for trading or trapping, and they carried long guns. This group could mean only trouble for the small band of women and children whose tipis clearly marked their presence on the hilltop. Full of foreboding, Kata Wi turned and ran back along the riverbed.

"Tanka!" she called. "The riders are white men. Too many, and they carry guns and come this way. We must tell the others."

Without waiting, she headed up the slope, away from the sparse cover of the trees to the group of tipis clustered in a circle on the ridge above, Tanka following close on her heels. But what could they do? There were no men here, only boys still too young to hunt. And the women had neither guns nor other weapons except for knives and hide-fleshers. She had the bow and arrows that her brother Chetanska, White Hawk, had made for her, but one bow would be of little use against the long firesticks of the white men. And of what use was one horse, and lame at that? The men had taken all the fit horses to hunt or to carry the slain buffalo, and the only one left in camp was White Hawk's stallion that had twisted his foreleg in a foxhole. With babies to carry and small children barely walking, they could never outrun the white men's horses. No escape was possible.

Breathless, the two girls reached the top of the slope where the women and older girls were at work within the circle of tipis while the younger children played nearby under the watchful eyes of their mothers. Kata Wi and Tanka shouted for their mother, startling the women at their work. Ina, their mother, stepped out of the largest tipi and met them in the center of the circle.

"Many white men are riding this way," Kata Wi said in a rush. Her words hung in the stillness of the afternoon like the dark clouds that portend a storm.

"They are riding like the wind!" Tanka added in a breathless voice. The other women clustered around.

"They come with firesticks and they follow the river. They are already near the bend."

Kata Wi's mother gazed at her intently, an unaccustomed frown puckering the smooth, bronze skin between her dark eyes. She did not speak. For the first time in the passing of many seasons, Kata Wi felt fear fasten on her throat like a coyote's teeth around the neck of a prairie dog. "Ina," she said softly, "do you think these men are looking for me?"

"Perhaps, my child," Ina said at last, and Kata Wi saw fear reflected in her eyes. "But we have no time to hide and no place to conceal you. We must prepare to meet them. Stay in the tipi and cover yourself."

Kata Wi hurried into the tipi and closed the flap behind her, leaving a gap just wide enough to see through.

"They are coming now!" one of the women cried as she gazed beyond the crest of the slope. With trembling hands Kata Wi wrapped a blanket around herself so that one corner fell across the crown of her head, covering a mass of tangled red curls. She was a Dakota, an Oglala Sioux of the western Teton tribes, but she had also belonged to the white man's tribe in some distant past. But her memories of that time had grown dimmer with passing time as though veiled by the mists that rise from the river at dawn.

As seasons passed, she had come to think the white man's world had forgotten her as well. Until the summer before when a stunted, grizzled man had come to trade his blankets for dressed buffalo hides. She had always tried to stay clear of the few white men who rode through their camps, but this man had come upon her by surprise. Caught unaware, she looked up to find sun-bleached blue eyes staring at her. She found them strange, disturbing even, and wondered if that was how Tanka and White Hawk felt when they looked into her eyes.

Turning her head away from the man's gaze, she had dropped her eyes, knowing their color would betray her, knowing, too, that he had marked them well. She sought refuge in the tipi until he rode away. It was not so easy to hide her foreboding at the trouble this man had promised in the intensity of his gaze.

And now this strange gift of foreknowledge that the Sioux called "hearing the spirit's voice" was telling her the men were coming to reclaim her. Outside, the women gathered the children to them, pressing them close against the folds of their soft deerskin dresses.

A man shouted from the bottom of the hill and she heard horses trotting up the slope. A group of men appeared over the crest of the ridge. The women moved together in twos and threes, shielding the children behind them. No one spoke. Only the sound of the wind in the cottonwoods by the river and the nervous whinny of White Hawk's horse broke the silence.

Through the open slit of the tipi, Kata Wi watched and listened. Her scalp tingled as if her hair that her father called "burning" was truly aflame. Eight men rode toward the cluster of women. One of them led a ninth horse without a saddle or rider. The men's white faces were clearly visible and reflected the light of the sun that began to pale during the Moon of the Falling Leaves. Kata Wi remembered faces like those from long ago days. She wanted to close her eyes against the faces, but she could only stare as if the spirits had turned her flesh to stone. A baby wailed, and the young mother lifted the infant from the pack on her back and put it to her breast.

The leader of the men dismounted and approached the women and children. Although a black wide-brimmed hat slanted low over his forehead and shaded his face, Kata Wi saw a thin white scar rip across one cheek and disappear into a ragged fringe of beard below his mouth.

"We want your white girl," the man said. He spoke in Dakota, the Oglala Sioux dialect, his voice ringing harshly in the silence. "*Wicincala ska*. White girl," he repeated. No one answered. In the dimness of the tipi, Kata Wi took a step backward and felt the coyote's teeth grip harder.

"Wilson, get down from there," he ordered in English to one of the horsemen. With a start of recognition, Kata Wi heard the language she had not heard or spoken for so many passings of the seasons. The words wove themselves into the Dakota words that by now were more familiar than those the white man spoke.

"Start looking," the leader said to the man called Wilson. "We got no time to fool around."

Wilson strode to the first woman, grasped her chin roughly with one hand and jerked back her head to inspect her face. He spat on his thumb and drew a wet mark on her cheek as though he found the copper of the flesh dirty and hoped to find a whiter flesh beneath. Kata Wi looked down at her hands clutching the edges of the blanket and knew that the skin, although darkened, was not the deep bronze of those born of Sioux blood.

"Squaw," the man said with contempt to the woman and moved to the next. Kata Wi buried her hands deep in the folds of the blanket. The women and children neither moved or spoke.

"*Wicincala ska*." Again the leader spat out the words. He reached out and grabbed a young boy by his hair, holding him with the blade of his knife pointed at the boy's throat. His mother cried out and reached for her son, but the man knocked her to the ground with one swing of his arm.

Kata Wi knew them well, had often told the boy, Sitting Crow, stories with the other children, had visited the tipi of his family and gossiped with his mother, Little Moon. They had gathered food together and dressed buffalo skins. It was Little Moon who had taught her to sew designs of porcupine quills. They were friends. She could not bear to see them harmed. Sitting Crow whimpered softly but still no one moved.

The leader gripped the boy tighter. *"Wicincala ska.* Bring her or . . ." He slashed the knife upward, holding the blade against Sitting Crow's forehead while his other hand gripped the boy's black hair. The blade glinted in the sun. Although Little Moon slowly rose to her feet, she did not raise an eye toward the tipi.

Drawing a deep breath, Kata Wi pushed open the flap and came forward through the clustered women to stand before the two men.

"Yelo yi," she said, telling them in a firm voice that it was she who was the *wicincala ska,* but her eyes hugged the ground.

Behind her, Ina cried out. Someone else began to sob. She was sure it was Tanka, but dared not look at her. She felt the scarred man's eyes search her face. She gazed at the dirt and trampled grass in silence, not wishing to confront the man's cold eyes.

"Look at me," he commanded in Dakota and slapped her so harshly that her eyes flew upward. She looked him full in the face, staring at the scar that sliced his cheek with its stark white line.

"Well, I'll be damned," he said in English and grinned suddenly. "Look here, Wilson, eyes as light as the sky above your head. I sure never seen no gray-eyed Injun. I think we caught a nice white pigeon, even if she does look like just another dirty squaw."

One of the men called impatiently from his horse. "Make sure she's the Porter girl, Matt, or we won't get our money!"

The meaning of the white man's words wove more quickly now into Dakota. Someone was paying these men to find her. But who? To bring her where? The man had said "Porter." In some long-ago time she had known that name . . . and other faces, but the images were blurred. Who was seeking her? A father and a mother she had long since thought dead? Was it possible they still lived? If not, what others? The fragment of memory whirled. Another sister . . . and a brother, too. Might one of them be searching for her even now?

Behind the two men who stood on the ground, she saw the others shifting on their horses.

"Hurry it up, Matt," one of them barked.

"Yeah, let's get goin', Matt. We sure as hell don't want to meet up with them braves."

Each word the white men spoke carved deeper into the granite of her memory.

"What's your name, girl?" Matt asked her in English.

Her name. She knew these words but would not give this man the satisfaction of her knowing. In silence she watched a tremor of anger cross his face, jiggling the scar on his cheek like a leaf on a tree.

"*Token eniciyapi he?* What's your name?" he asked again, his voice lashing at her like a whip.

She looked him full in the eyes. "Kata Wi," she said in a firm voice.

"Burning Sun, eh? Where'dja get that name?"

Without warning, he grabbed the edge of her blanket, yanked it from her head, and lifted a hank of her hair. "Just what I thought—red hair, and curly, even if it is all smeared with buffalo grease." He gave her hair a sharp pull, making her wince with pain. She bit her lip to keep from crying out. "What's your other name, girl?"

Kata Wi clenched her lips.

"What's your real name?" he asked in English. "The name you was born to? Is it Rachel? Rachel Porter?"

Rachel. Rachel Porter. That was her name, and the sound of it swept away the mists that for so long had clouded memory. She felt unfamiliar tears wet her cheeks and closed her eyes against them.

"Rachel." She whispered the name aloud, remembering another time and the young girl Rachel whom long ago she had left so far behind. Slowly she spoke in English, and on her tongue the words felt strange and sounded somehow forlorn. "I am Rachel Porter."

"Then you're the girl we want. We're here to take you back!"

2

Rachel Porter leaned against the rail of the steamboat *Yellowstone* and watched the dark water of the Missouri River churn in a froth of brown and white across the bow. During the night cold winds from the west had swept across the plains, driving the warm autumn air before them.

The day was chilly and damp, the air heavy with moisture. The mist, like her jumbled thoughts, swirled around her in gusts. Nothing seemed clear to her now. Nothing except the fact that the white men had taken her to Fort Tecumseh and delivered her to the captain of the ship anchored at the landing. Somewhere downriver her father awaited her. That much the captain had made clear to her after he paid the men their money.

The white men had also wanted horses but had to leave empty-handed when they discovered only White Hawk's hobbled stallion tethered on the slope. She was thankful that Morning Star, her own sorrel mare, was safe with White Hawk on the hunt.

Rachel had spoken only once during the long afternoon's ride to Fort Tecumseh, when they had stopped along the widening stream to rest their horses in midafternoon.

"How did you know to find me?" she asked Matt in Dakota, refusing to speak the language that now sounded harsh to her ears. He answered her in English.

"Sam Greenleaf, the trader, he seen your blue eyes. He told Gus at the trading post there be a white woman here. Gus spread the word downriver." He spat into the river, sending an arc of tobacco juice as dark as the flowing water. "Your pa hired me to find out if you was his daughter and bring you back. We scouted out the tribe's camp and waited 'til we saw the men leave on the hunt. It were easy."

He spat once more, but this time the brown juice erupted in a spurt of dust beside her bare feet. Rachel stood her ground. "I can't figure," he said, "why any man'd want a girl that's no better than a squaw."

Those were the last words they had spoken. She hoped she would never have reason to speak with or see him again, but she wondered if she would ever again hear the voices of the family and friends she had grown to love during the passing of seven winters. No escape seemed possible. She could not have outridden the eight men who brought her to the fort, and now the treacherous river kept her prisoner on the ship. She dared not look back. She could only look ahead, and she must hold to the comfort that Ina, Tanka, and the others were unharmed.

She stood alone at the rail. Since the men had pushed her without ceremony onto the ship two days earlier, no passenger had approached her. Although she had slept alone in a wooden bunk in a cabin beneath the deck, hunger had driven her to join the other passengers when they gathered for meals in the large room at the center of the boat. But no one had acknowledged her presence, and she had seen their guarded looks.

Now she felt the curious eyes rake her back as they passed along the deck behind her. Did they think she might attack them if they came too close, or was it her buckskin dress and leggings that made them stare? Or perhaps the quilled band she wore around her head to bind her hair? She had only the clothes on her back, but she had taken pains to tan the skins to supple softness and sew the quill designs of birds and running deer.

The women on the ship wore long flowing dresses of woven cloth that covered their legs to their feet. The tops of their dresses bound their breasts and squeezed their waists. How could they draw an easy breath or ride a horse in such clothes? Or climb a tree to gather pine cones and nuts still hanging on the branches? The skins of her dress and leggings were soiled from hard wear and the long ride, but they were soft and warm and fell from her shoulders in a loose fold.

The women talked in voices that were lost in the wind, but now and then a word or two drifted to her as she stood beside the rail. "Heathen . . . dirty squaw . . . injun whore . . ." The words jabbed at her heart like quills.

She wondered about the family that now awaited her

arrival somewhere along the riverbank and how they would feel about her return after so many seasons had widened the distance between them. Surely they would welcome her. Why else would her father have sought her? And what of her mother? Neither the man Matt nor the captain had spoken of her mother.

Pictures of the time before she lived with the Sioux wove through her mind, but they were like the veins of mica in the high caves, sometimes glimmering in the darkness, sometimes fading before she could see them clearly. In one bright gleam she saw waves breaking along a rocky shore, a caravan of wagons following the paths of many rivers that joined one to the other without end until the open plains stretched before them, green and rolling like the other distant waves. Then a fireplace built of stones hauled from the bluffs along the river, so big that in summer, before suppertime, she and her sister and brother could hide behind the neatly stacked logs. Her sister was Leah, her brother James John. Jamie, they had called him.

She stared at the river that lapped at the ship's hull with a strong brown tongue. As the ship's bow sliced the surface of the water, the foam swirled outward forming white circles that floated on the brown water. Closing her eyes as the Shaman had done from the center of the ceremonial circle, she let the pictures rise from the darker waters of her mind and float within the circles swirling on the surface.

In front of the stone fireplace stood a heavy wooden table with rough edges that sometimes poked splinters into careless fingers. At the far end a man, her father, sat with folded hands and bowed head, speaking prayers. He wore a black coat and the firelight danced on the curve of his high forehead that ran into neatly trimmed hair the color of the flames.

Across from him, framed by the fireplace, the shadowed face of her mother leaned forward, already marked with fine lines etched by weariness and the dry prairie winds. Her still hands rested on the broad curve of her abdomen, heavy with a child soon to be born.

Rachel had often wondered about that baby not yet born. Did she have another brother or sister? What might this child make of her, a sister never seen, who now spoke the Dakota tongue with greater ease than the language of white men?

"Rachel Porter?"

Quicker than the flash of an eagle's wing, the voice summoned her back to the deck of the ship. Rachel turned to face a woman the age of Ina. The hood of a cloak covered her head but revealed a face with small features and skin reddened not by the sun but by the sharp bite of the wind. Her hands held a small bundle of clothing.

"I am Rachel Porter." She spoke the words slowly. But of course the woman would know this. The captain would have told them all about her while awaiting her arrival.

"We thought . . . I was wondering . . ." The woman looked away from Rachel's questioning eyes and raised her head as if searching for words in the blowing wind.

"We will be landing at St. Joseph very soon now," she continued. "We . . . I thought you might like to change your clothes before we arrive. I have some of my daughter's clothes here . . . just a few things I thought you could use . . ." Her voice faltered. "Here!" she said suddenly and thrust the bundle of clothes into Rachel's hands. "Take them, my dear. It will go easier for you, I think." Before Rachel could reply, the woman turned and hurried toward the stern of the boat. Rachel was aware of the other passengers' curious eyes fastened on her.

She looked down at the bundle, fearing now what awaited her at this strange place called St. Joseph. For the passing of seven winters she had lived as a Dakota. How would they expect her to look? A hard knot tightened her throat and moved downward, settling behind her ribs with a dull ache. For the first time since she had ridden away from Ina and Tanka, tears rose and blurred the scene before her, blending the stern faces of the passengers and the stark outlines of the landscape along the riverbanks into a single, shapeless cloud.

The ship held her captive. Escape was impossible except by plunging into the churning waters of the cold Missouri, a path that could lead only to her death. But if she must meet whatever awaited her at the next river port, at least she would not pretend that Kata Wi had never lived.

She blinked away the tears and followed the woman toward the stern, forming the words inside her head until she could feel them ready on her tongue.

"Lady," she began, and the woman looked up startled. Her hair, the color of autumn grass, was pulled tight behind her head, but little wisps blew free around her face.

"Yes?" she responded, and the wind took the word and wafted it skyward.

"Lady, I thank you for your kindness. But I must not wear these clothes."

"Must not? Whatever do you mean, 'must not'?"

"I have fine clothes. I shall keep what I have." She held out the bundle, but the woman did not take it.

"Child, you mustn't flaunt your Indian ways," she said not unkindly, "or it will go hard on you. We've heard the stories from other women who have come back. We know how heathen braves use captive women. Why would you wish to offend your people by reminding them of what you have been?"

Although the wind was cold, Rachel felt her face flame.

"I remind them of nothing except that I have lived at a great distance for the passing of seven winters!"

"Look at yourself. How can you think they wish to see you this way? They remember the girl that was taken from them, not a young squaw who has learned strange ways and lived a life of squalor and . . . who knows what else?"

"I have lived with a kind family! I am who I have always been!" She wanted to cry out against what this woman said and what she had seen in all their faces and heard in the whispered words, but the words twisted and caught in her throat. The bundle dropped to the deck.

"Perhaps I was wrong," the woman said sadly. "Perhaps new clothes cannot hide a heathen soul. In any case, it's too late now. That's St. Joseph up ahead, off the starboard rail."

Rachel spun around. The *Yellowstone* was swinging around a bend in the river, and in the distance on the east bank stretched a cluster of frame buildings. The great paddle wheel churned the water into a foamy wake as the ship turned from its midstream course and steamed toward the landing.

"For goodness sakes, child," the woman said at Rachel's elbow, "at least put on some shoes." She knelt and rummaged in the bundle of clothes on the deck and pulled out a pair of ladies' boots. She thrust them into Rachel's hands. "I don't know why your feet haven't turned to ice by now," she said and walked away.

As they approached the landing, a handful of people milled along the shore, waiting for the ship to dock. Behind them the town appeared full of movement. Horses trotted along the streets pulling carts and wagons loaded with wooden barrels and burlap-wrapped bales, followed by men and women who seemed in a hurry. Now and then a chicken or goat wandered into the street followed by a scampering child who chased the wayward animal out of sight. Cats and dogs seemed to come and go at will.

As she watched the hurried movement of the busy market town, Rachel felt the sharp twin teeth of fear and regret gnaw at her stomach. The men and older boys of the tribe would be returning to the camp from the hunt by now, full of stories to tell and brave deeds to relate. What would her father and White Hawk do when they heard the white men had taken her? Would they mourn her loss in a ceremony for the dead or would they set out to find her? And how would that be possible in the midst of a busy town full of people? These whites would watch her closely, of that she was sure!

Anger rose and mingled with the fear. She raised her arms overhead and flung the boots far out into the river. As she watched them sink beneath the waves, she reached into a deep pocket sewn into the front of her dress and pulled out a pair of soft deerskin moccasins. Bending, she slipped them onto her feet.

The great wheel slowed and died in a final churning of brown water. The steamboat's whistle blew three long blasts, letting the whole town know that the *Yellowstone* was at the dock bringing mail and supplies as well as passengers from the north.

Rachel watched the people on the landing, a blur of passing forms and faces. The dockhands shoved the gangplank onto the deck and the passengers collected their bundles and bags, preparing to disembark.

In front of her she saw the woman who had given her the clothes cross the gangplank to shore. She turned once to look at Rachel, then stepped onto the landing and disappeared among the milling people. Rachel watched the last passenger walk down the gangplank.

A member of the crew appeared at her elbow. "End of the line, Miss," he said in a gruff voice. "You get off here." He took her by the arm but Rachel shook off his hand and slowly moved toward the gangplank. Her legs felt as heavy as the stones hewn from the great bluffs that stretched above the river to the north. What would she do if no one came to meet her? Worse even than the dread of meeting her other family was the specter of being left alone to fend for herself in this bewildering place.

She searched the faces on the dock, but no one seemed to be seeking her. At the far edge of the landing a solitary man dressed in black stood unmoving among the bustle of people. His head was bare. The skin of his face was drawn and gray. Through the thin mist that curled up from the river's edge his hair above the high forehead was a glimmer of red-gold streaked with gray, like the dying flames of a fire banked deep with ashes.

Rachel's heart stopped. With trembling hands she pulled her blanket close around her and slowly walked across the rough planks of the dock to within a few feet of where the man stood.

The man gazed intently as the last of the ship's passengers moved past him one by one. Then he turned and walked toward the lowered gangplank, coming face to face with Rachel huddled in the safe cocoon of her blanket.

He glanced at her once, and a look of faint distaste tightened the deep creases that ran along the bridge of his nose to the down-turned corners of his mouth. Rachel felt the wooden planks rock and sway under her feet, and she willed her knees not to buckle beneath her. He started to pass her by, then stopped and looked, and his eyes searched the contours of her face. She remembered those fierce pale eyes gazing out across the top of a great black book. Slowly she released the edges of the blanket and the rough garment fell away from her head and dropped to the wooden planks beneath her feet. He stepped toward her.

"Can it be? Rachel?" His voice rasped, and he spoke her name again. "Is it Rachel?"

"*Yelo yi.*" As though from a great distance of time and space, she heard her own voice speak the Dakota words, and the man's face tightened and closed. The landing shuddered and swayed as though floating on a surging tide of water. "It is I, Father," she said. "I am the one you call Rachel."

3

On the short journey from the wharf to their house at the far edge of town, Rachel's father spoke only briefly of the events of the last seven years.

"You will find things greatly changed, Rachel," he said, looking straight ahead up the road.

As you have found me greatly changed, she thought, and wondered if that was his thought as well.

He let the reins fall slack, slowing the wagon. "I am sorry to have to tell you this. Your mother is no longer with us." He paused, staring straight ahead as though searching for words in the road. After a moment he continued. "She died giving birth to your brother Daniel, shortly after the attack on the fort. I would have spared you this news for a while but . . . well, you see, I have taken another wife. I thought it best to tell you before we arrived home."

The news of her mother's death bound her heart, but the grief was more for the loss of another mother than for an individual who was now only a shadow. Her father would expect a reply, but words would not come. She felt curious eyes turned on her from all directions along the street and kept her own eyes fastened on her hands folded in her lap.

"But I have good news as well," her father continued. "They found your Aunt Sarah last spring among the Comanche. Your Uncle Nathan has taken her to live in Jefferson City. Now it only remains for us to find your brother James John. And find him I will, by the will of God, if it's the last thing I do in this lifetime."

His voice cut through her like the wind from the north. He flicked the reins, urging the roan mare to a trot, and spoke no more.

A blur of names and faces whirled before Rachel's eyes. Feeling faint with confusion and loss, she shivered, not knowing if it was his words or the cold wind that chilled her most.

As they turned into a narrow dirt lane, a fine rain began to fall, and Rachel pulled her blanket tighter around her shoulders. The lane led to a small shed behind a larger frame house. In the gathering darkness, lights flickered behind narrow paned windows, revealing a flurry of movement within. A small pale face glimmered behind one of the windows, then disappeared almost before she could be sure she had seen it. The reins slackened across the horse's back, and the wagon came to rest before a wooden lean-to attached to the back of the house.

"We're here, Rachel." His voice broke in the twilight, and he coughed to clear his throat. "This is your home." Before she could reply, a door burst open and three figures catapulted out of the light.

A whirlwind of voices swallowed her.

"Rachel . . . at last!"

"Help her down."

"Bring her inside . . . she'll be soaked to the skin."

". . . such a long journey."

The words tumbled together in a confusion of sounds she could no longer separate. Hands grasped her, leading her into the lighted room where a great fire burned at one end, and the same hands guided her to a bench before the fire and gently pushed her down. The blanket lifted from her shoulders.

"Hush, child," a new voice said, "let the poor girl catch her breath." One by one the voices stilled until the room was silent. "Daniel, go help your father with the horse. Leah, stoke up the fire and lift off the stew."

Leah. The name wound out of the past. Her sister's name. Rachel looked into the round pale moon of the face floating above her near the fire and knew she was beholding a young image of the mother who had died. That face had also bent over a black pot hanging on an iron hook, the skin flushed and rosy from the heat of the fire, the hands lifting the corner of an apron to wipe away little rivers of perspiration, just as Leah was lifting it now.

Leah turned to meet Rachel's eyes with a smile.

"Leah," Rachel said slowly, hearing her own voice as though carried by a current from a great distance. "My sister Leah." The white face hovered, then dropped in a rush to hide in Rachel's lap while white arms wound around Rachel's bent knees.

"Oh, Rachel," Leah cried, lifting her face wet with tears. "I thought perhaps you had forgotten me!" She held Rachel's cold hand tight in her own, and Rachel was grateful for her sister's warm touch.

The rest of the evening dissolved in a confusion of names and faces, strange smells and tastes. The boy they called Daniel came in from the darkness with her father and watched her shyly from across the room, finally edging his way closer to finger the beads on her dress.

Her father's new wife, Nina, moved about the room, preparing food for the evening meal. Although she appeared frail, her movements were strong and fluid like water flowing in a narrow stream, unhurried but constant. Slight of build and much smaller than Ina, the two women seemed close in age, but Nina's hair was the color of bleached summer grass coiled softly around a pale, narrow face.

In the center of the room sat the great oaken table Rachel had remembered from so long ago. Before they ate, her father sat at one end with folded hands and spoke from the great black book.

"Amen," Rachel heard the others say together, and then the food was passed around the table. Although she had not eaten since the night before, she took no food for herself. She was afraid to pick up her knife and fork, afraid clumsiness might betray her unfamiliarity in using them.

"You must eat, Rachel," her father said, and his voice made her start.

"Some bread and milk will do for tonight, Tobias," Nina said quickly, cutting a crusty loaf with a knife. "Have some bread, Rachel, still warm from baking." She thrust a good-sized piece into Rachel's hands.

The bread tasted warm and fresh, not too unlike the flavor of sun-ripened nuts. Rachel washed it down with the cold milk that Leah held out to her in a cup. The feel of food in her stomach and the warmth of the fire burning in the hearth made her eyes grow heavy.

"Let's get the poor child to bed," she heard Nina's voice, as soft as the light rain against the window.

"She must bathe first," her father replied. "Look at her." The expression Rachel had seen on the wharf pulled at his features now, and the deep voice echoed what was mirrored in his face. "Look at those clothes. They're filthy." It was difficult to protest against that look and voice. The words tripped her tongue and escaped before she could say them.

"Oh, yes, a bath and then bed," Nina said. "Leah, get out the tub. See if the water's hot."

"Daniel, come with me," her father said, moving toward the door. "Time to bed down the animals for the night." Rachel felt a cold draft sweep the room as the door opened, then closed behind them with a bang.

Leah pulled a copper tub in front of the fire and emptied the kettle of boiling water into it, adding two buckets of cold water from beneath the sink.

"Let's get these dirty things off her," Nina said, taking Rachel by the arm and helping her to her feet.

"I—am—not—*dirty.*" Rachel protested with all the force she could muster, and the loudness of her own voice startled her in the hush of this fire-lit room. "I will keep my clothes." She wanted to strike out against all that was happening to her, but her tired body betrayed her, too limp to hold the anger that sapped what little strength she had left.

She saw Leah lift a sympathetic face, but Nina did not seem to hear the anger. She began to strip off the clothes Rachel had made with so much care and pride. "A bath will make you feel better," she said with a cheerful smile. "You'll see. Then to bed. You've been through enough for one day."

Leah's look of concern and the kindness in Nina's voice melted Rachel's anger. Rain was falling, deepening the night. She was in a strange land with nowhere to go. Tonight she must do their bidding. But her time would come.

She stood in silence as Nina removed the last of her clothes and Leah lifted each foot and slipped off the moccasins. Holding Leah's arm to steady herself, Rachel stepped into the tub and sank into warm water up to her waist, surprised at how pleasant it felt. Her weary muscles responded to the gentle lapping of the water against her skin, and for a moment she closed her eyes and let the past days' events slip away one by one until time had stopped and she was back on the banks of the Bad River, standing in the warmth of the midday sun.

Nina lifted one of her arms out of the water and began to scrub hard with the soap and a coarse cloth.

"Now, we'll see how pretty your sister can be!" she said, smiling at Leah on the other side of the tub.

Rachel felt her skin tingle and burn under the moving cloth. Dipping the cloth in the tub, Nina swished a stream of warm water over the soapy skin.

Rachel lifted her arm from the water and stared in amazement. In the light from the fire, the washed arm gleamed pale and white next to the darker skin of her other arm. For a moment she stared at the two arms together, wondering if it would be this easy for them to wash away all the layers of the past, all of her seven winters with the Dakota. A sense of loss flooded over her, bringing unexpected tears.

Through the blur of tears she heard Nina's cheerful voice. "Now your legs," she said. "Then we'll wash all that buffalo grease out of your beautiful hair!"

After the bath they dressed her in a long nightgown. She resented the garment, but the cloth felt warm next to her skin and she held it close against her.

"Now, Rachel, just look at yourself!" Nina said and held a round piece of polished metal in front of her face. "She's a sight for sore eyes, isn't she, Leah?"

"Rachel, you look beautiful!" Leah said, and Rachel heard admiration in her voice.

Rachel gazed before her and saw the mirrored image of a girl she barely recognized staring back out of eyes the color of a winter sky. Instead of being bound behind her head and held smoothly in place with a layer of buffalo fat, her hair floated in a flaming cloud of curls around her face. The skin of her face glowed pink from the scrubbing Nina had given it. It was the face of a white girl. Sick at heart, she turned her eyes away, closing them against the truth of what she had seen reflected in the polished surface.

The door opened and a gust of wind swirled dried leaves across the floor.

"Come see what a pretty daughter you have, Tobias!" Nina called gaily and turned Rachel to face her father. His eyes traveled the length of her body but gave no hint either of Leah's warmth or Nina's delight.

"She is better. This house will never harbor heathen squaws, no matter what the blood." Although he directed his words to Nina, Rachel felt them like the sharp point of an arrow. They echoed the words she had heard on the *Yellowstone*.

Anger churned deep within her. She was no heathen squaw but daughter of a Dakota chief, and she would never wish to be otherwise! But her mind was too tired to form the words, and she held the thought inside.

The strain of the long journey, the heat of the fire and the burden of her father's words combined to weigh on her eyes. Although she fought to keep them open, the craving for sleep suddenly engulfed her, and she sank to the bench.

"We must get her to bed," Nina's voice urged. "Leah, go with her. I'll wash up tonight. Daniel, it's time for you to go, too. Now scoot."

Rachel felt Leah's arm encircle her waist. She rose from the bench in response, following Leah out of the warmth of the bright room and up dark, winding steps that led to a small room lit only by the candle Leah carried.

"This will be our room now, Rachel." Rachel tried to respond but could only nod her head. "We will share a bed, too," Leah said, leading her to a wooden bed piled high with a stuffed pallet and blankets. "I hope you don't mind."

Rachel shook her head and lay down on the strange bed and let her eyes fall closed. She felt Leah tuck the blankets around her. Long ago her mother's hands had moved in the same way.

The last she heard before sleep engulfed her was Leah's voice, whispering close beside her. "I'm so happy, Rachel, so happy to have you back home." A puff of breath blew out the candle. Darkness entered the room and led her, floating, toward sleep.

A short time later she awoke to the faint sound of a door opening. Hushed footsteps approached, and she heard a rustling not far from the bed. Then the door closed again, softly. She lay half-awake, listening, then faded back to sleep.

In the middle of the night, she awakened more fully, feeling the strangeness of the room and the bed beneath her. Beside her she heard Leah's soft breathing and remembered she was in her father's house. But sleep did not come so easily again. The bed was soft, making her bones ache, and it creaked and rustled when she moved. She was used to the firm feel of the earth beneath her.

Silently she rose and pulled a blanket from the top of the bed. She lay down again on the wooden floor, wrapping the blanket snugly around her. Lying on her back in the darkness, she felt the hard boards beneath her and listened to the familiar sounds of the night. The rain murmured to her through the roof above her head. In the distance a mourning dove lamented for its lost mate. An owl called in reply.

You are not alone. You are not alone, its voice seemed to say. Then the darkness moved inward, and she slept.

4

At daybreak, broken fragments of troubled dreams pursued Rachel into wakefulness. She felt herself once again on the wooden deck of the *Yellowstone,* which in her dreams was drifting down a river so wide she could not see the banks. Slowly she opened her eyes in the hazy light just breaking across the window at the end of a strange room tucked under a roof.

The sound of soft breathing above her reminded her that she shared this room with her sister Leah, older than her sister Tanka by the passing of two winters.

If only Tanka could have seen her the night before. How amazed she would have been to see her sister bathing in a tub with hot water in winter! Tanka would be arising now in the dim light of the tipi to help Ina prepare the early meal before her father, Waoka, and White Hawk went out to hunt or practice with their bows. Even now they might be speaking of her, wondering where she was. How Waoka loved to laugh! She had seen him angry only once, when the brave who took her captive first brought her to the Big Horn Mountains where the tribe was camped that summer.

Waoka had been angry with the young brave and had given him four fine horses in trade for her, a price of immense value. It was Waoka who had given her the name Kata Wi, Burning Sun. Unlike the young brave, who had often pulled her by the hair, Waoka had touched her hair with a gentle hand and laughed aloud. The day Waoka had taken her to live with him and his family was the first day she could recall clearly. But perhaps her memories of them would begin to fade as quickly as her recollection of the white man's world had faded during her time with the Dakota. Perhaps their names and faces would also dim with each new moon. Worst of all was the thought that *they* might forget *her*. She shivered in the gray morning light.

Above her Leah stirred among the covers on the bed. Silently Rachel climbed out of the blanket she had wrapped around her the night before and spread it across the top of the bed just as Leah awoke.

Leah looked up and stretched out a hand in greeting. "It's nice," she said, smiling sleepily at Rachel "to wake up and see you here."

Her smile embraced Rachel, for the moment warming the chilly room. "It will be a fine day, I think. The sky is not red," Rachel replied, careful to say the proper words.

Barefoot she walked across the cold boards to look out the cramped window of the sleeping loft. A fire burned in the yard below. Beside it, her father stood feeding her clothes to the flames that devoured them.

"*Hiya!* No!" she cried, but the heavy wooden walls and panes of glass made her words a prisoner in the narrow room. She rapped on the glass but her father seemed not to hear. She beat her fist against a wooden mullion until she was afraid the glass might break, but he did not look up. She saw him hold her dress above the fire and let it drop. In horror she watched the flames lick the edges of the soft deerskin.

Not the dress she had made from the deer White Hawk had shot and skinned just for her and that she had worked on so long to tan and sew with polished quills! He had no right to burn her clothes!

He stooped to pick up her moccasins and held them over the fire.

"*Hiya!*" she cried again and flung herself away from the window and down the narrow winding stairs. As Rachel burst into the room, Nina looked up from the fire.

"Rachel, what's the matter?" she called after the fleeing figure. Without pausing to answer, Rachel dashed through the door and ran headlong into her father on the back stoop.

He reached out a hand to stop her but she pushed past him and ran toward the flames that were already dying. A smoldering heap of burning embers was all that remained of her clothes. In her bare feet she stood helplessly watching as the flames consumed the last vestiges of her deerskin moccasins. Her eyes blazed more fiercely than the fire as she turned to confront her father.

"Those were *my* clothes," she said, and her voice shook with anger. "You had no right . . ."

"In this house I have every right!" his voice thundered in return. "I'll have no flaunting of your Indian ways here! You will learn to be one of us again." He turned to the door and opened it. "Now get back upstairs. And don't come down again until you are properly clad." He held the door, glaring at her from the stoop until she entered and made her way up the winding stairs to the loft.

Leah stood at the window where she had watched the scene below.

"Don't worry, Rachel," she said, touching Rachel's shoulders with her fingertips. "Nina has brought you fine new clothes. See there?" She pointed to a neat pile of washed and mended garments that their father's new wife had placed on a wooden chest. Beside the clothing stood a pair of black boots and, next to them, a pair of heavy shoes.

Sick at the thought of what she had just seen below, Rachel dressed herself slowly. The clothes felt heavy and rough and did not give her warmth. She watched Leah lace up her boots but left her own sitting beside the wooden trunk. If only he had not burned her moccasins! She shivered again in the cold that had settled under the eaves and, barefoot, followed Leah down the winding steps.

Her father and the boy Daniel were already seated at the table in the center of the room. Leah greeted her father, bending to place her lips on his forehead. Rachel stood at the bottom of the steps and wondered if she, too, were expected to touch the strange man who was her father with her lips in this manner. His eyes traveled the length of her body, and he spoke to her before she could move.

"Yes, those clothes fit you just fine. You look quite presentable."

Standing straight and tall before her father, Rachel drew a deep breath. "My clothes—" she began again and saw his hand rise to silence her.

"—are not acceptable now," he said. His hand lowered to rest, palm down, against the wooden tabletop. "But you must wear something on your feet. It won't do to go without shoes here."

"You had no right . . ." she persisted.

This time the hand rose and fell to the table with a bang. Leah jumped and Daniel's eyes widened in alarm.

"Enough! Daniel, go and fetch your sister's boots!"

Without a word the boy slipped by her and clambered up the steps, reappearing in a moment with the pair of black boots, one in each hand. He held them out to Rachel shyly, glancing up at her through thick dark lashes that screened round eyes, gray like her own.

"Here, Rachel," he said, handing them to her, and then added, "they are very good for walking on pebbles."

She wanted to protest further, but this child's words of encouragement made her smile. For now she would let the protest wait. Her sharp tongue and quick temper had sometimes caused her trouble even among the Dakota, and it was not only her flaming hair that had won her the name Burning Sun. She must be careful now to curb her temper. As long as she was a prisoner here, she would try to make the best of it. She could see clearly that opposing her father would only make her life more difficult. Until she could think more clearly what to do, she must be careful to watch her tongue.

"*Niye wopida eciya*. Thank you, Daniel," she said and sat on the bottom step to pull the boots on her feet. When she stood up to walk, they felt heavy and cumbersome, and the laces trailed behind on the floor. "Now, Daniel," she said, speaking slowly and squatting so that she was at eye level with the boy who stood watching her, his eyes wide with wonder, "will you help me tie the laces like yours? If you help me know your ways, I will teach you Dakota ways. We both can learn."

"Help her with her boots, Daniel." Rachel looked up to meet her father's smoke-colored eyes that stared at her without warmth. "But as for learning Indian ways"—his voice sliced across the room with a sharper edge—"there will be none of that here. Do you understand, Daniel?" Although he spoke to the boy, Rachel felt his eyes fixed upon her. "We want no reminders of Indians in this household. It is a rule not to be broken—ever."

"Yes, Father," Daniel said softly and bent over the boots.

Rachel saw his small fingers tremble as they picked up the laces. She clenched her lower lip between her teeth to hold the angry words in check. Her white father had no right to burn her clothes nor to ask her to forget her life as a Dakota. His rule was a law she could not obey. But she would hold her peace for now. Everything in its own season. That was the law of Wakan-Tanka, Infinite Spirit of the Universe whose laws could not be broken by any man, not even her father.

"Rachel will do just fine." Nina spoke in a firm voice from in front of the fire. "The boots are for everyday, child, the shoes are for Sundays and special occasions.

They may feel strange now, but you'll be happy to have them when the snow falls. Now come and have your breakfast. There will be plenty of time to learn all of these things. First things first."

After breakfast their father left for duties at the church where he was pastor. Rachel stood at the wooden sink laden with dishes, her arms up to the elbows in hot water. She gazed out the little window that overlooked the yard. A blackened ring clearly marked the spot where the fire had burned. A pile of dead ashes was all that remained. Daniel was poking at the cold embers with a stick, hatching a web of lines in the gray surface.

Rachel's head spun from so many strange new encounters. She had bathed in a tub in winter and slept, for a while, in a bed. She had porridge for breakfast and had eaten it with a spoon. She was wearing woven clothes and high-laced boots. With Leah beside her, she was washing the dishes from the morning meal with a lump of soap and water pumped from the ground with a wooden handle.

She lifted her arms from the water and saw the skin gleam in the clear morning light. A white girl's skin. She felt the anger churn again deep in her stomach and swallowed hard to contain it. The dream that had haunted her sleep the night before, the dream of being lost in a landscape with no familiar shores, floated on the surface of the soapy water.

She lifted a plate from the sink, dipped it in a pan of clear water and handed it to Leah to dry.

Nina was right. First things first. Her turn would come.

Outside, Daniel stooped to retrieve something from the ashes. For a moment he peered at what was in his hand, then stood and ran toward the house. The door burst open and he stood on the threshold, excitement shining in his blue eyes.

"Rachel, look what I found!" he cried and ran to her with outstretched hands, his shyness forgotten.

In the palms of his small hands lay two charred objects, her stone flesher and a scorched piece of deerskin with the likeness of a soaring hawk embroidered in polished quills. It had been part of the pocket that held her moccasins and the scraper.

Unmindful of her dripping arms, Rachel dropped to her knees beside her brother and gently lifted the objects from his hands. She traced the outline of the hawk with a wet fingertip, remembering how long it had taken her to fashion it.

"Is it part of your dress, Rachel?" Daniel asked, sadness deepening his child's voice.

"Yes, Daniel, and my flesher. We use these to clean skins for our tipis and our clothes."

"Will you show me how sometime, Rachel?"

"You know what Father said, Daniel!" Leah's shocked voice warned from above.

Rachel had not forgotten the stern warning, but the look of hopeful expectation in the boy's eyes made words come quickly.

"Yes, someday I'll show you," she said, and returned the smile that lightened his face. "Someday we'll skin a deer, and I'll show you how the Indians prepare a hide."

"Rachel, how would you dare? Father will be so angry!"

Rachel looked up at her sister. "I said I would teach him Dakota ways, and I shall. It was a promise I made. And it will help me not to forget."

The boy's arms reached around her neck, hugging her tight, and she felt the soft skin of his cheek press against her own. A warmth she had not felt for days moved through her and her own arms reached out to embrace the slight body before her.

"Thank you, Daniel," she whispered. She buried her face in the collar of his blue homespun shirt and felt a consoling hand pat her gently on the shoulder.

"Don't cry, Rachel," the small voice said quietly in her ear. "Don't cry. It's all right. I'll take care of you."

5

I n the dim light of the cold stone church, Rachel felt Leah shiver beside her on the hard pew and press closer to her for warmth. Beneath the fullness of her linsey-woolsey skirt, Rachel eased the shoes from her feet and wiggled her toes to circulate the blood and warm them.

Today marked the first day of the Moon of Hairless Calves, the first of November. During the moon's half cycle since her coming, she had learned to tolerate the high black boots Nina had given her, but the stiff Sunday shoes pinched her feet and made them grow cold and numb.

Rachel curled her toes, wondering why anyone would want to wear stiff shoes instead of boots made of winter buffalo hides tanned to supple softness and worn fur inward to cushion and warm the feet. If only she had thought to bring those boots with her! But then her father would have burned them with her other clothes.

A brazier full of blazing coals had been placed in the center of the aisle before the service, but by now the coals had burned to gray embers. Little clouds of white steam puffed from her father's mouth as he spoke to the gathering. In front of him, propped on a wooden stand, was the great black book they called *The Bible*.

Her father's droning voice floated aloft with the smoke from the dying embers and hung among the cobwebs in the wooden rafters. Although by now she could more easily follow the path of the words and understand their meaning, the words he spoke this morning bewildered her. They summoned no vision like the Shaman's chants. Her father's words spoke of *sin* and *penance, wrath of God, seeking the way to salvation*—words that meant nothing to her. They only made her dwell on how long the voice had pressed onward and how hard the edge of the bench was digging into the back of her knees.

She glanced beyond Leah to Daniel who had been in the world as long as she had lived as a Dakota. Daniel sat with his eyes half-closed, playing with a piece of string in the shelter between his knees. At the end of the string dangled a black beetle that was trying to crawl up the rough wool of his pants.

Next to him, Leah sat motionless, hands folded in her lap, eyes fastened intently on the man who seemed to hover over them like some great black bird. Now and then Rachel heard a small sigh escape Leah's parted lips.

The words stopped. The people knelt to pray, and finally the service ended with the singing of a hymn. The voices were thin in the cold air, but the music and words gripped Rachel.

> Rock of ages, cleft for me,
> let me hide myself in thee.

Let the water and the blood
From Thy riven side which flowed . . .

The meaning of the final words blurred—what was a "riven side"?—but around her each note ascended, lifting her in the image the words awakened, transporting her into the deep labyrinth of crystal caverns high in the *Paha Sapa,* the Black Hills. Near the summit the cave's mouth opened as a single fissure in the rock, summoning those who dared to enter and seek the vision of spirits that dwelled within the deep abyss. That aged rock had opened for her and offered a glimpse of the mysteries secreted in the dark chasm.

The notes of the hymn floated upward in a circle of sound. For the first time since her return, Rachel felt life begin to flow within her veins.

The hymn ended. Her father raised his hand to speak the blessing, then stepped down and passed through the rows of benches to take his customary position at the front of the church. As he stood in the open door, the congregation filed down the aisle, greeting him briefly before stepping into the cold November morning.

Outside, Rachel stood apart, watching the people mingle and converse with ease. The women were dressed in what Nina called their "fancy go-to-meeting clothes," except for the three Porter women, who wore dresses of plain cloth such as they had worn all week. Her father called fancy clothes a "vanity" and the "devil's work," although she wasn't sure what he meant by those words.

Nina had given her a hat to wear that tied in a large

bow and scratched her chin. At first she had protested wearing the hat, but Nina stated firmly that hats were always to be worn to church and most decidedly on Sundays.

"It's no good arguing with her when she uses that voice," Leah had whispered to Rachel later. "And when her mouth becomes a straight line, she means business and no nonsense about it."

In the short time she had lived with this family, Rachel had learned the truth of Leah's words. Although Nina usually spoke softly and with good humor, upon occasion it was useless to argue with her.

All the women wore hats to church. Some were plain like her own, but others were trimmed with bright-colored flowers and ribbons. On Dakota ceremonial days, it was the men who wore the headdresses to show their status in the tribe, bonnets made with special care by the women who decorated them with feathers and beads until they gleamed and shimmered in the sunlight like bright birds. Dakota women never wore hats, and wouldn't Tanka and Ina look amazed, wouldn't they laugh to see her now!

Outside the church, the men stood in groups of five or six, talking quietly among themselves. The women clustered and broke apart, forming small groups of twos and threes in a pattern of continuous movement like a dance.

Through the milling throng, Rachel saw Nina standing with her father at the top of the steps. Leah was nowhere to be seen. As the women came and went, Rachel caught snatches of their conversation.

". . . and sometimes they cramp up so bad, it keeps me up all night."

"Too bad there's not a better cure than oil of camphor. I'd rather have the cramps."

". . . posting the banns next Sunday and not a moment too soon."

"Like as not, the next thing you know they'll be . . ."

"They do say she . . ."

Like the chatter of magpies, the women's words rose and fell around her. A woman standing nearby looked familiar, and when she turned Rachel recognized the woman from the *Yellowstone* who had offered her clothes. After a moment's hesitation the woman approached.

"I'm sorry if I seemed to be staring," she said, "but aren't you the girl on the ship, Rachel Porter?"

"Yes, I am Rachel Porter," she replied, and for a moment it was as though she were back on the ship and the woman was coming to offer the clothes again.

"I thought so, but I couldn't be sure. There's such a change. I'd hardly have thought it possible in just two weeks." Rachel stood in silence, wondering what she should say to this woman. If only Nina or Leah were beside her now, but with barely a pause the woman continued.

"I'm Mrs. Penniman." She regarded Rachel through a veil that dropped from the brim of her hat across the tip of her nose. "I see you have changed your clothes after all, my dear. And such a pleasant surprise. You really are a very pretty girl. One would never have known."

"Yes, ma'am," Rachel said, parroting the phrase Daniel often used when speaking to Nina.

"Perhaps some day you might come to tea."

"Yes, ma'am. Thank you, ma'am." Her tongue felt awkward and thick. Would she ever learn how to talk at ease with these people?

"I shall drop a note to Mrs. Porter, and we'll arrange a day. It will be good for you to meet other young women in the town, don't you think?"

"Yes, ma'am. Thank you," Rachel started to repeat, but before the words were fully formed, Mrs. Penniman had turned to join another woman passing by. The two walked away together.

Across the churchyard, Leah suddenly appeared behind a cluster of women and threaded her way to Rachel's side.

"Let's start home," she said, hooking her arm through Rachel's. "It's too cold this morning to stand about." She led her across the yard to the path that cut through the tiny graveyard, a shortcut to the road out of town.

Rachel thought it strange that white men buried their dead deep in the ground, enclosing the spirit as well as the body in eternal cold and darkness. The thought made her shudder. Since her return to her white family, the vision of her own death had often appeared both in her dreams and waking thoughts.

"If I die," she said to Leah in a low voice, "don't let them put me in the ground."

"Goodness, Rachel! Why would you think of dying? We've just gotten you back. We're not going to let you go again!"

"I think perhaps others don't feel as you do."

Leah stopped beside one of the carved stones and turned to look into Rachel's eyes.

"You mustn't think that. When you've been here longer, you'll see. Everyone will forget what's past."

Rachel shook her head. "The words I heard on the ship . . ."

"What words?"

"Heathen . . . dirty squaw . . . other words I did not know."

"How could anyone call you 'heathen' when Father is a minister of the church?" For a moment Leah was silent as they stood at the edge of the small burial ground. "Perhaps, it would be better, though, if you didn't speak outright of such things as not being buried. They sound strange to us . . . to people here."

Leah paused a moment, intent on her thoughts, a puzzled look puckering her white face with only the tip of her nose rosy from the November frost. "But Rachel," she asked, "what *do* Indians do with their dead, if they don't bury them?"

"Some Indians do, but under a pile of rocks, never deep in the ground. The Dakota raise the dead to free the spirit."

"*Raise* the *dead*? Oh, Rachel, don't let Father hear you say that! Only Jesus could raise the dead, like in the story of Lazarus in the Bible."

Rachel shook her head, trying to make the jumbled pieces fall into place. "I mean this," she said and lifted her arms high above her head, palms upward. "The Dakota raise up the dead to a high place, the branches of a tree or a mountaintop, where the spirit can take wing and fly free of the body."

"Oh, *that* kind of raise!" Leah raised her arms as well to show she understood, then let them drop to her sides. "Our mother is buried, Rachel," she said softly.

"In the ground?"

"Yes, right over there." She pointed to a stone at the far corner of the small graveyard. In silence the two girls approached the stone that curved in an arc. Rachel saw letters and numbers carved on the face of the stone. Because she still grieved the separation from Ina and Tanka, she had not often thought of her white mother's death, but it seemed strange to think of her buried in the cold ground.

"Our father told me she died a great distance from here, as long by horse as the journey of the sun's full circle. The time it takes to ride from . . ." Rachel paused, seeking the white man's words, "*wihinapa ekta wii-yaye* . . . from sunrise to sunset. How does she come to be buried here?"

"Didn't Father tell you? She died right after the attack on the fort when Daniel was born. He came too quickly. The bleeding wouldn't stop. No one could help. We buried her at the fort, but the Indians had burned most of it and no one wanted to stay . . . to be reminded. So we all left."

Leah rubbed her mittened hand gently over the top of the stone. She was silent and Rachel saw tears rim her eyes, but after a moment she continued.

"After we came to St. Joseph and settled here, Father

and Uncle Nathan drove a wagon back to the fort to bring Mother's casket here. We buried her twice." She blinked back the tears and looked up at Rachel with a quick smile. "But at least Daniel lived. After the Indians had taken you and Jamie and Aunt Sarah, he helped to fill the emptiness. Oh, Rachel!" she cried, flinging her arms around her sister's neck, holding her tight. "It was awful after the three of you were taken! Father was like a madman, and then when mother died so soon after, I thought he might . . ."

Leah's voice faltered. Her words startled Rachel. It was the first time she had thought of the suffering this family must have felt during the time she was gone, or that bad *wakan* might have come to them. *Wakan* was all-powerful. A man with good *wakan* lived a truly blessed life, but when he suffered bad *wakan* . . . She shuddered at the thought.

"I fear for this family, Leah," she said, speaking slowly, seeking the right words. "I think perhaps bad *wakan* has followed me from the north and now dwells in our house."

"Bad *wakan*? What is that, Rachel?"

"It is all that is sacred and mysterious in the universe. It is the power of Wakan-Tanka."

"Who is Wakan-Tanka? Is he like Jesus?"

"Wakan-Tanka is the The Great Holy-Mystery, Spirit of the Universe. For people who offend Wakan-Tanka, terrible things happen."

"What kinds of things?"

"A woman might no longer bear children. Or she might die while giving birth, like our own mother. Children sicken and waste away from fevers no medicine can cure. Men lose the power to hunt and find food." Rachel lowered her voice to a whisper. "Bad *wakan* even allows a brave to lose his scalp in battle. When this happens, it means the loss of his magical powers and, worst of all, loss of his eternal soul. The family that suffers bad *wakan* is truly cursed!"

"Oh, Rachel, you mustn't think that of this family!"

Rachel hugged Leah, knowing that their brother Jamie had never been found, fearful of what might still await them all. Over her sister's shoulder she gazed at the stone that marked their mother's burial place, noting the lines and circles carved in the granite, words and numbers that told a story unknown to her. Reaching out, she traced the lines, feeling the smooth chiseled edges beneath the rough skin of her finger, but the meaning of those strange words remained buried within the stone. How could she survive in this strange world when so much of it was lost to her?

"Leah," she whispered, "tell me what the stone speaks." A cloud passed over the full moon of her sister's pale face.

"What it speaks? Stones don't . . . I'm sorry, Rachel, I don't know what you mean."

"The words on the gravestone. I don't know what they say."

"Oh, Rachel," Leah cried. She grasped her sister by the hand, her eyes wide with amazement. "You mean you can't *read* what's written there?"

"No, I cannot."

"But that's not possible! I mean, you used to read so

well. You loved to read, and you were teaching Jamie, too, just like a regular schoolmarm. We taught him reading from the Bible. You must remember that."

"I remember the book called *The Bible*. I can see some of the stories in that book that our father speaks from. But I don't remember how to . . . I cannot read the words."

"Then I will teach you! We'll begin right here, and we'll have a lesson every day!" Leah's dark eyes shone with excitement. "See," she said, pointing to marks on the stone, "these are the numbers. One, eight, aught, six—that's the year Mother was born—and one, eight three nine—the year she died." Rachel traced the smooth grooves with her finger, repeating the numbers Leah had spoken.

With a stick Leah scratched the numbers from one to ten in the loose dirt at the foot of the grave, saying the name for each as she wrote it. Rachel repeated them in order, then took the stick to copy her own numbers beneath the ones Leah had written. The lines wavered but clearly resembled the ones above. Rachel spoke the numbers again and looked up at Leah, laughing in triumph.

"See, Rachel," Leah said, hugging her, "you'll be reading again in no time!"

Rachel caught Leah's excitement. "Now show me the words!" She knelt by the grave while Leah spoke and pointed to each word engraved on the face of the stone.

"*Martha Porter*—those words say her name." Rachel slowly repeated them after Leah, carving them into the surface of her memory as her fingers traced the outlines of the words.

"*Loving - wife - and - mother.* . . . *For - now - we - see - through - a - glass - darkly - but - then - face - to - face.* . . . That's a saying from the Bible," Leah said.

Again Rachel felt the letters that formed the words. "*Now we see . . . through a glass darkly.*" She felt the sounds of them on her tongue. "I like those words. They speak what I feel. So much of what has passed remains full of shadows. Truly I see through a glass darkly."

"'*But then face to face.*' Don't forget that part, Rachel. Of course, the Bible means it won't all come clear until after we die. But that won't be true this time. You'll see. We'll start tomorrow after chores. Since it's my job to give Daniel his lessons, I can teach you together. It will be much more fun that way—just the three of us!"

Rising from her knees, Rachel stumbled on the hem of her skirt and clung to the top of the gravestone to steady herself. The November wind bit through her cloak. If only she still had her warm, fur-lined robe that no wind could penetrate!

The earlier elation dimmed. She was grateful for Leah's words and for her offer of help. But still the dark shadow of bad *wakan* seemed to linger over the land, over her, and over this family that had reclaimed her.

6

The sun broke through the clouds directly overhead as the two girls hurried down the road toward home. They were late for the noon meal and their father would be angry that Nina had to prepare the dinner alone. When they had passed the last house, they saw the road empty before them.

"Let's run!" Rachel called and bent to slip off her shoes. The two girls picked up their skirts and ran the last few hundred yards to the front gate. They darted across the wooden planks that bridged the muddy yard, Leah's heavy shoes clattering on the boards that bounced beneath their feet.

Breathless and windblown, they arrived at the front door just as it opened before them. Their father stood beneath the lintel, a frown creasing the broad forehead above eyes that reminded Rachel of ice floes floating on the rivers at the last turning of winter.

He glanced at her feet, and his mouth tightened in that thin line of disapproval that had become all too familiar in the past two weeks. Bracing herself to meet his anger, she was surprised by his words and the evenness of his voice.

"Leah, Rachel, we have a visitor. He's just returned from Jefferson City and has come to welcome Rachel home."

Rachel looked at the young man who stepped from the shadows to greet them. He was not many years older than White Hawk. She stared at his smooth, clean-shaven face, unlike those of most of the white men who lived in St. Joseph which were full of hair. She thought of White Hawk and the first time she had encountered him when he returned to the camp shortly after Waoka had taken her from the renegade brave.

At thirteen, only three years older than she, White Hawk had already been accepted into the tribe's band of hunters. When Waoka brought her to meet him, he scowled at her, but soon after became her protector and her teacher. He taught her to ride bareback and helped her break the wild pony Waoka gave her for her own.

When she outgrew the pony, White Hawk searched out the finest mare on the plains, captured her and gave her to Rachel as a gift. She had named the mare Morning Star. The horse was her most precious possession, and she never rode the mare without thinking of White Hawk. If only he were here now, ready to welcome her within the circle of his blanket and hold her in his encircling arms.

Rachel looked again at the young man who stood before her dressed in calfskin breeches and a checkered shirt under a brown vest. He looked strangely familiar. Taller than her father by several inches, his height and the width of his shoulders would almost fill the doorway where Rachel still stood. Wide-set hazel eyes looked at her from under a shock of hair, redder than her own but straight and wiry, that fell across a broad forehead. A spattering of freckles deepened the color of his skin.

"Rachel," Leah turned to include her in her smile of obvious pleasure. "You remember Peter, Peter Ellsworth."

Holding out his hand, he stepped forward to greet her with a handshake.

Rachel stood motionless in the doorframe trying to remember this man from the past. Peter Ellsworth. The name, too, was familiar, but it faded into the patchwork of the other names and faces she had met since her return.

"Welcome home, Rachel," he said, but when she didn't reply, his broad smile began to fade, and his words, like his hand, hung awkwardly in the space between them. "It's good to have you home," he said after a moment. She lifted her hand and he grasped it in his. His palm felt rough and warm, and his fingers swallowed hers within their firm clasp.

"Surely you remember Peter, Rachel!" Her father's voice broke the silence. Peter released the hold on her fingers. "He was with us at the fort when the Indians came. It was Peter who went out to meet them. Surely you recall that!"

She remembered a young man—no older than she now—riding through a stockade fence at the fort a day's journey south of St. Joseph, while she waited to bar the gate behind him. In the distance a band of Indians, painted for war, approached the fort on horseback, searching for food and horses that were not in the fort to give. It was Peter who had been left on guard at the fort that summer morning while the other men worked the farms a mile away. She had watched him ride out alone to tell the Indians they had neither food nor horses to spare. He had hoped to keep the Indians occupied while the women and children escaped through the back gate to hide in the thick groves by the river. The gate had closed behind him and she swung the heavy bar across it. It was the last time she had seen him.

"I remember," she said as the scene slowly shifted into the present, to the kitchen in St. Joseph. To see him now, standing before her, seemed an act of good *wakan,* the most sacred magic. "Peter Ellsworth," she said regarding him with wonder. "I thought you were dead. At the time of the attack, I was certain the Indians would kill you."

"I was pretty certain they would, too! I never could figure why they didn't scalp me out there in the fields. It still surprises me."

"But now I know Dakota do not kill for no reason!" Although her angry indignation was plain to hear, Rachel didn't care. "*Killing* is not held sacred by the Sioux nations, only *coups,* only taking great risks in battle!" Peter's eyes narrowed and tightened just as her father's did when she spoke of her Dakota family or the Oglala tribe.

"Rachel, I'll have no more of that heathen talk!" Her father's voice lashed out. "And why are you barefoot again? Put on your shoes!"

Her eyes blazed back at him, but this time her lips did not speak what she felt. For a moment she regretted her hasty retort to Peter. It did no good to defend the Indian ways here. White people could not believe she spoke the truth. Peter Ellsworth was like her father. Let him think the worst if he would.

She turned away and bent to slip on the shoes she still held in her left hand. Carefully she tied the laces in two neat bows.

Behind her Peter's voice filled the silence. "Well, whatever the reason, I'm happy to be alive." His voice softened, and Rachel felt the words directed to her. "What made me happiest, though, was hearing that you were still alive, too. We were beginning to fear the worst. But when they found your Aunt Sarah alive last spring . . . well, it gave us new hope, didn't it, Tobias?"

"I never gave up hope, nor faith that the good Lord would return both Sarah and Rachel. Now with His help, we'll find my son James, too."

"Your aunt sends you her love, Rachel," Peter said, coming to stand beside her. Leah's eyes followed him wherever he moved. "She was both happy and thankful to hear you were back."

"How is Aunt Sarah?" Leah asked.

"That news can wait until we eat," Nina said, coming in from outside with a jug of milk, followed by Daniel who carried a basket of eggs. "You're very late. We've been waiting dinner on you. Now help get the food on the table. Peter, you sit there, next to Leah."

They gathered around the table, folding hands and lowering their heads while their father spoke the grace.

". . . and we most heartily thank You," he finished, "for the presence in our midst of Peter Ellsworth and for his continued safety. Amen." The others echoed the "amen" while Rachel, knowing her father's eyes would be upon her, mouthed the word. Each time he came to the end of the grace, he watched her to be certain she joined in and reprimanded her if she failed to repeat the response.

Rachel noted the food as she passed each dish on to Daniel who sat beside her: a head of cabbage from the root cellar under the lean-to, cooked until soft with dried savory and salt pork; potatoes boiled in their jackets; rabbit stewed with wild onions; bread baked from coarse-ground cornmeal. In the center of the table sat the pitcher of cow's milk. Only the rabbit cooked with onion tasted familiar. It was tender and succulent. Nina was a good cook, almost as good as Ina. They were alike in many ways. Even their names were similar.

"You set out a fine meal, Mrs. Porter," Peter said, but his eyes feasted on Rachel. She dropped her gaze to the table. The spark that danced in his hazel eyes reminded her once again of White Hawk. He would be squatting on his haunches beside a stream or mounted on his horse, perhaps eating a bite or two from his parfleche, the pouch that carried all plains Indians' food. He would be eating buffalo jerky or pemmican that Ina had made early in the fall from powdered meat, dried ground berries, and buffalo fat. She had helped Ina grind the meat and berries at the end of summer. Would White Hawk be thinking of her as he ate?

She glanced again at Peter from under lowered lashes. He seemed at ease with this family and ate with obvious relish. Dakota men rarely took time to return to camp at midday, but white men seemed always to return home to eat, like her father who ate his noon meal here every day.

"Tell us your news now, Peter," Nina said as they were finishing the meal. "You have word from Sarah and Nathan?"

"I stopped with them for one night on my way north from Arkansas." He paused, searching in the pocket of his shirt. He pulled out a long splinter of wood and poked it between his teeth. "Sarah's ailing. She caught a cold and can't seem to set it by."

"A cold? That doesn't sound too serious," Nina said as she rose to clear the table.

"You wouldn't think so. But she's getting too thin and she tires easy." He placed the toothpick back in his pocket. "She's just kind of "—he searched for the right word—"wasting away. Nathan's had every doctor in Independence to look at her, but they can't tell what's wrong. He wanted to take her to Hot Springs, for the waters, but she wants to come home—here where her family is. She said—and these are her very words—'I especially want to see Rachel.'"

Rachel felt his gaze on her again but kept her own eyes lowered. This man with his laughing eyes somehow made her uncomfortable, although she wasn't sure why. Perhaps he reminded her too much of White Hawk. She stood up to help Nina clear the dishes and knew his eyes followed her.

"They'll be coming before Christmas, or as soon as Nathan sells his business. Maybe within the month."

The face of her aunt appeared bright and unshadowed in Rachel's memory. She saw herself as a child, long ago when they lived by the ocean, before the long journey across the prairie, that boundless sea of grass. Aunt Sarah was her mother's sister, her favorite relative, as full of laughter as her father was stern. Although her father forbade dancing, sometimes Aunt Sarah had showed Rachel the steps she danced at parties. She sang the tunes as she waltzed around her kitchen. There had never been a bird as quick and light as Aunt Sarah twirling around the table with her skirt held high, her boots skimming the boards as lightly as a feather in the wind.

The thought of Aunt Sarah coming to St. Joseph filled Rachel with happiness. Aunt Sarah would know how she felt. She would not expect her to be someone she was not, could not, be. "*Niye wopida eciya,*" she whispered softly, directing the words to the powerful spirit of Wakan-Tanka. "Thank you, and Amen." For the news of her aunt she was truly thankful. But Peter had told them that Sarah was wasting away. The shadow of bad *wakan* still hovered over this family like the wings of an eagle searching for prey.

But Aunt Sarah would be coming soon, coming to St. Joseph. There would be two of them then.

"I have other news," Peter was saying. "Just before I left Little Rock, word came that a group of captives had been discovered in Texas among the Comanche." Rachel's father looked up from the table, a strange look of longing softening his sharp face. He said nothing but looked at Peter with full attention, waiting for him to continue. "A squad of militia is escorting them to Little Rock, ten captives in all, two of them boys about thirteen or fourteen."

"Then either might be Jamie!" Rachel thought she heard a tremor in her father's voice.

"Yes, but no one knows for sure who they are. I guess neither one speaks any English. I understand there's a few women in the group as well . . . in pretty bad shape from what I heard." He glanced at Rachel, a strange look she had not seen before bathing his face in a wash of color. He looked down at his hands, studying the fingers that revealed a thin line of black beneath each nail. "They had been . . . I mean, they had . . ." He struggled for words. "They had been badly used," he finished in a rush. "One of them couldn't speak at all."

"When will they get to Little Rock?" her father asked.

"Today or tomorrow, depending on how fast the women and children can ride."

"Then I must leave tomorrow as well. I can be there by Thursday if all goes well. Nina, send word to Bishop Thomas to come for Sunday service this week." Nina nodded in reply and went quickly into their bedroom to pack the necessary clothes in a saddlebag.

Rachel sensed she was watching a scene that had been enacted many times. All those years that she had been gone—this must have been the way her father had responded to every rumor of the discovery of captive children. How many times had he set out in search of her, only to discover that the girl he sought was not among them, that he stood face to face with someone else's daughter? And the same was true of Jamie. How many times had this journey in search of him been made in vain? At the thought of what might await him again, her heart ached for this stern man. And what awaited the women and children riding into Little Rock?

Her father rose and shook Peter's hand. "Thank you for the news," he said, and his eyes stared beyond them to the gray sky that stretched across the far horizon. "Keep an eye on my family, Peter, if you will. I shall be home by Sunday after next, if not sooner. No matter what the outcome, before two weeks have past, I shall know if they have found my son."

7

In the days that followed, after chores were done and the sunlight blazed into the kitchen through the western window and caught the tiny dust motes floating in the air, Leah spent an hour with Rachel and Daniel, teaching them how to read and write and figure numbers. The lessons progressed swiftly. Rachel was intent, determined to remember the skills she had forgotten, and Daniel was a bright boy.

They sat at the oaken table in the center of the kitchen, Leah at the head in their father's place, with Rachel and Daniel on either side. Sometimes Leah used the hymnal as a reader. She first taught them to read the hymn that had reminded Rachel of the glistening caves of the Black Hills.

> Rock of ages, cleft for me,
> let me hide myself in thee.

Word by word they read the verses, saying the letters and sounding the syllables until whole words emerged, then lines, and finally a whole sentence or stanza. Both pupils shouted with elation when they could read the hymn from beginning to end.

"Now it's time to practice writing," Leah said, smiling to show her pleasure. Rachel was amazed at how quickly Daniel learned and was quick to praise him.

"You'll be the smartest of us all, won't he, Leah?" she said, giving the boy a hug that brought a smile of pride and pleasure to his face. "And I'll be the dunce of the family. It's hard to believe I could have forgotten so much!"

"The writing takes more practice," Leah said, "We only have one slate so you'll have to take turns. Daniel, why don't you read the words to Rachel first and let her write them."

Daniel picked up the hymnal and read the first line without a pause.

"Not so fast!" Rachel laughed. "You're way ahead of me!"

Slowly she formed the words, struggling with her piece of chalk, writing each word letter by letter as Daniel read them. Leah stood above her, now and then taking her hand to help with the outline of a difficult letter.

Before they knew it the hour had ended and the sun had drifted below the window ledge. Both sides of the slate were covered with writing. Rachel gazed at the neat rows with pride. Wouldn't Tanka and White Hawk be amazed to see her writing and reading! White Hawk could draw the likenesses of the birds and animals that roamed the northern plains, and Tanka was one of the best at decorating with porcupine quills and beads, but neither of them could read or write. She would like to be able to teach them herself one day.

Nina stoked the embers on the hearth, adding two logs as the kindling ignited and burned. Dusk was the nicest time of day. After work was finished, they gathered together in the kitchen to prepare the evening meal. With Father gone, the small house seemed more relaxed. Supper sometimes rested at the edge of the hearth as the four of them laughed and chatted. It was hard not to think about how long it might be before his return or to notice how pleasant it was with him away. Two weeks at the most, he had said. They should make the most of the time, Rachel thought.

Leah closed the hymnal, signaling an end to the lesson, and Daniel picked up the slate and chalk.

"Show me Indian writing," he said, holding them out to Rachel. "Please, Rachel, write some Dakota words."

Rachel glanced at Nina scraping carrots into the sink. She hadn't seemed to notice his request.

"I can't, Daniel," she said, and disappointment shadowed his blue eyes. "The Sioux don't have writing. Not writing like this," she explained pointing to the words she had written on the slate.

"Don't the Indians have *books*?"

"No, Daniel, no books. Sometimes they draw pictures on buffalo hides to keep records of the passing seasons or battles they have fought or the movement of buffalo herds across the plains. But they don't have books."

"You mean they don't read?" His look of amazed disbelief made Rachel laugh.

"No, no reading either."

"Don't they have lessons to do?" Such a marvelous thought made his eyes grow wide with envy, and even Leah's mouth dropped open at the wonder of it. At the sink Nina chuckled.

"But how do they learn things?" Leah asked.

"They learn by watching and by listening," Rachel said. "Children are taught to listen when the elders speak. And the children listen to the stories."

"Stories?" Daniel's wide eyes lit up.

"Yes, stories like we're learning to read in the Bible. But the Indians don't *read* them. They tell the stories, and the children listen and learn. And when they grow up, they will tell the stories to their children. And that way the stories are never lost."

"Tell *me* a story, Rachel!" Daniel begged, throwing his arms around her neck to hold her in the chair. "Tell us an Indian story."

"Daniel, you know what Father would say. You don't want to get Rachel in trouble, do you?" Leah said.

Nina set a wooden bowl full of carrots and turnips in the center of the table and sat across from Leah. "I don't see any harm in telling a story," she said, handing Leah a paring knife. "Leah, you scrape the carrots, I'll slice the turnips, and Rachel can tell us all a story."

Daniel's arms slipped from Rachel's neck. He climbed into her lap, and she held him loosely in the crook of her arm, feeling his small body settle against her shoulder.

"I'll tell you the Dakota story of how the world will finally end." She looked down at her brother's face and saw expectation mirrored there. A half-burned log crackled and split, sparks exploding into the chimney while the flames leapt upward in pursuit.

Within the flames patterns formed. Rachel gazed into the fire and waited for the image that would bring the story she sought. She rested her hands lightly on her knees, palms downward, fingers stretched toward the fire as though to touch the shifting pictures. Except for the crackling of the logs, the room was hushed.

The pictures shifted within the colors of the flames, from the crimson of the western sun to the indigo of nightfall.

Slowly, softly she began. "Imagine for a moment that it is night," she said, closing her eyes to see the darkness that comes after sundown before the moon begins to rise.

"Everything on earth is still, silent, and unmoving. The world is lit only by the silver net cast by the moon, stars, and a fire that burns in the darkness.

"Near the fire, an old Indian woman sits in the moonlight and sews with bright porcupine quills on a strip of buffalo skin. By her side a dog lies, watching, waiting. Over the fire a kettle of herbs boils." Another log broke and a shower of sparks erupted. In her lap Daniel shifted slightly. Rachel let the images settle.

"Every now and then," she continued, "the old woman rises, lays down her work, and goes to the fire to stir the pot of herbs. While she is tending the pot, the dog lifts his muzzle and pulls on the thread she has been sewing, unraveling all of her work. Then the old woman returns from the fire, picks up the skin, and sews once more.

"This has been going on for thousands of years. As

fast as the Indian woman sews, the dog unravels. For if she should ever complete her work, at that instant the end of the world will come.

"So say the Dakota wise men."

As she ended the story, Rachel sat without speaking. How often she had heard this story told when children gathered at end of day to listen to an elder of the tribe as he repeated over and over what the Dakota believed to be the most important lessons in life, the great mysteries of earth and sky.

In her lap Daniel sat without moving, head pressed against her shoulder. The sun had dropped beneath the horizon. Beyond the window, an orange glow swept across the framed stretch of purple sky. Darkness nestled in the lap of the rolling fields beyond the house. Inside, the room was bathed in silence as the four sat around the table and watched dusk close in.

Nina rose and brought a burning taper from the fire to light the lamp that hung above the table. As she held the taper to the lantern, the wick blazed, enclosing them in a soft circle of light.

A surge of homesickness swept over Rachel, a longing to be with the people who told these stories and knew them to be true, her people. Tears sprang to her eyes, but she saw Nina watching her across the table and she blinked them away.

"What is it Rachel?" Nina said, coming to stand beside her. She put an arm around Rachel's shoulders. "What is making you feel sad? We want to help."

"Of course, we want to help!" Leah echoed, and Daniel looked up at her, nodding in agreement.

"I know that," Rachel said, making an effort to smile. "It is just that they suddenly seemed so far away." No one questioned who *they* were, and she hesitated, examining more deeply what she was feeling. "And I am afraid," she continued slowly.

"Afraid of what, Rachel?" Nina asked in her soft voice. "Surely you aren't afraid of us. There is nothing here to fear."

"Being here is not what I fear," Rachel said, searching for the words that would say what she felt so they would understand. "I am afraid of losing all I have known for the past seven winters, just as I lost so much of what I knew before I was taken by the Sioux brave." She clasped her hands. "I know now that it is easy to forget the way when you stray too far for too long."

"Isn't marking a trail the best way not to lose it?" Nina asked.

"But how can someone mark what is only remembering?"

"Why, exactly the way you have been doing here this afternoon."

"Of course, Rachel!" Leah broke in. "You can *write* everything you saw and did. You can practice your writing and at the same time tell everything that happened. You can write a book. That way you'll have it to read whenever you want to remember a part of it."

"And put in lots of stories," Daniel said, tugging at her sleeve to make sure of her attention, "like the one you just told!"

Their words sent shivers along her spine. They were right. She could write about everything that happened while she was with the Dakota. She could tell about her family and the tribe. What better way to narrow the distance between them? Every day she would write about them and bring them a day's journey closer.

She would tell about her life on the plains and the life of the tribe. She would write about the Black Hills and the crystal caves. She would even tell the story of her journey north with the brave to the Big Horn Mountains where Waoka had found her. It was not the story she wished to remember, but it was part of her story and could not be left out. And some day, a long journey ahead in time, she might let this white family see what she had written. They could read her book and learn the things she could never speak.

And of course Daniel was right. She must tell the stories she had heard so often. They would be the most important part of her book. That way she would never forget them.

"You are right," she said to the three faces that waited expectantly for her response. "That's exactly what I'll do! I will write it all, if you will help me, Leah."

"Of course I'll help you!"

"Me, too, Rachel. I can help, too," Daniel chimed in. "I'll help you write the stories."

"We'll all help," Nina said, smiling at the three of them. "I'm glad that's settled. Now, who's ready for supper?"

8

The next week passed quickly. Rachel worked hard on her writing, practicing for the day when she would be ready to begin her book. And every afternoon, after lessons, she told another story of the Sioux, sometimes to Nina and Leah and always to Daniel.

Often in early evening, Peter Ellsworth appeared at their door, sometimes early enough to join them in supper. "Just to make sure you're all well," he said more than once. "After all, I promised Tobias I'd look out for you while he's gone."

"He might say he's looking out for us," Nina said one night after Peter had stayed until late in the evening, "but I think he's come a-courting. Only I can't figure which one of you he favors. I'm not sure he knows, either."

Rachel glanced at Leah and saw a blush wash her pale skin with rosy color, making her face gleam in the dying light of the fire. Leah's feelings lay close to the surface. It was easy to see that Peter was special to her. Rachel only hoped that Peter felt the same about Leah. But she was not unaware of how often his gaze followed her and how often he found some pretense to sit near her. She hoped that Leah hadn't noticed but she feared she had. In the past few days Leah had seemed quieter, less talkative with Rachel even when they were alone.

Rachel tried not to show interest in Peter, but it was hard not to respond to his attentions. She missed the easy friendships of the young men and women in the tribe, particularly White Hawk and Tanka. Peter had traveled many places, as far south as Texas, and all the way east to the Smoky Mountains. Rachel loved to hear him tell about his travels, the places he had been to and the people he had met, and she had many questions about the parts of the country she had never seen.

But often she found herself disagreeing with Peter and found it hard to hold her tongue. Sometimes they argued when he came to visit until Nina declared a truce and distracted them with a game or by asking Peter to play a song on the harmonica he always carried. He had a pleasant baritone voice and could always be persuaded to sing a song or two.

When he heard about her book from Leah and Daniel, Peter brought a quill pen and ink he had wheedled from the town schoolmaster, and he presented them to Rachel with a smile.

"Now you can write in style."

"Yes, if only I had something to write on." She held up the slate and smiled in return. "I think my book will have to be very short."

One evening in the middle of the second week since her father's departure, Peter arrived a little before suppertime with a half dozen exercise books. Leah saw him coming in the distance and hurried upstairs to change her dress. Daniel and Nina were in the shed milking the cow, so Rachel found herself alone with him.

"I brought you something," Peter said in the way of a greeting. "The children use these for their lessons. I thought at least they would be better than the slate." His fingers brushed her hand as she accepted the booklets he held out to her, and for a moment he did not withdraw them.

"Thank you," she said, feeling suddenly shy with the gift. Paper was dear and hard to come by. He must have paid a good price to get so much. She looked at the paper in her hands but felt Peter's eyes locked on her. "You mustn't bring any more," she added in a rush of words. "I know it's very costly. I have more than I shall need, I'm sure."

"Don't worry about the cost," he said. "I traded a few hours of my time as a surveyor for it, so it didn't cost me a penny."

"Perhaps not, but it cost you wages." She made herself look up into his eyes that were only inches away. They crinkled slightly at the corners.

"Oh, this isn't a gift," he said, smiling. "You owe me for it."

"Then you must take it back, for I cannot pay."

"It's not money I wish."

"What then?" she asked sharply and backed away a step. "I have nothing else to pay you with." For a brief moment the cruel face of the brave who had taken her captive flickered before her eyes in the flames of the fire. She saw him again, standing over her in the clearing where they had stopped for the night on their journey north. Six other braves sat across the fire but would not raise their eyes to look at her.

The brave's face was faint now, his features indistinct, but she remembered the look she had seen in his eyes and shuddered at the recollection. "I can't pay you," she repeated, taking another step backward.

"Whoa!" Peter said, and the light in his eyes faded. "I don't want anything from you except to read some of your book. All I want is to learn about what happened to you. After the attack—well, I never knew anything except that you were captured by some Injun. But the paper's yours, even if you don't want me to read what you write on it."

"It's just that I can't be sure how it will turn out. Perhaps you can read some of it," she said, contrite at having mistrusted his offer but not knowing how to make amends. Would she never learn to respond less impetuously?

During supper Peter was polite but aloof and paid special attention to Leah, who glowed. Normally somewhat reticent, tonight she was animated and after supper consented to sing a song while Peter accompanied her on his harmonica.

"Let's do 'Come Fair and Tender Ladies,' Peter," she suggested shyly, and Peter was quick to agree. He placed the small instrument against his lips and swung into the plaintive melody without hesitation. Leah followed his lead, singing the words in a lilting soprano that was soft but true.

Come all ye fair and tender ladies,
Take warning how you court young men.
They're like the stars on summer's morning
First they appear and then they're gone.

Daniel curled up on the braided rug in front of the
fire and was fast asleep before the second verse began.
At the hearth, Nina popped corn in a long-handled pan
over the smoldering coals. As the kernels grew hot, they
ruptured in little spurts against the sides of the pan.

On the second verse Peter set aside the harmonica and
his baritone joined Leah in singing the words of the old
love song. Their two voices blended, filling the room
with the clear notes sung in harmony.

If I had known before I courted
That love was not so true and fine,
I'd have locked my heart in a box of golden
And tied it with a silver line.

It was clear to Rachel that he and Leah had sung
together many times. For an instant Peter raised his eyes
and met hers, but just as quickly he dropped them again
and gave his full attention to the words and melody.

When they came to the final verses, Peter's voice took
up the melody, the soprano and baritone blending as a
single instrument.

Oh, I am not a little swallow,
I have no wings, neither can I fly.

So I'll sit right down to weep in sorrow
And let my troubles pass me by.

Oh, don't you remember the days of courting
When you laid your head upon my breast.
You could make me believe with the falling
    of your arms
That the sun rises in the west.

Peter picked up his harmonica again to play and Leah repeated the first verse. Nina joined them, humming the harmony.

Rachel watched the three of them and felt as though she were standing outside in the darkness peering through the window at the bright scene within. It was like sitting at the outer edge of the ceremonial circle and hearing the mysterious chants of the braves as they sang and danced to honor Wakan-Tanka, the great mysteries of the universe and all living things on earth. Often during the ceremonies, before White Hawk was old enough to join the men in the circle, she had sat with him to watch. If only he were here now, sitting beside her as Leah and Peter sang together, she would not feel so alone, so outside the center of things.

When the song ended, the four sat in silence for a moment. With a sudden bustle, Nina passed the bowl of popcorn and the spell was broken.

"It's your turn now," Leah said, pulling Rachel by the hand. "Sing us an Indian song."

Daniel stirred on the hearth. "Sing an Indian song,

please, Rachel," he murmured sleepily without opening his eyes.

She glanced at Peter, but he played soft scales on the harmonica as though oblivious to the spoken pleas of the others. She wondered how he would feel if she sang a song of the Dakota tribes.

"I'll sing a lullaby," she said, "a song Dakota mothers sing to their babies. They wouldn't let me sing to them, though," she said, laughing. "They always said my singing woke them up. I don't have a voice like Leah's."

She took a deep breath, but before she could begin the sound of a horse's hooves pounding up the road through the darkness broke the silence. Leah peered through the window.

"It's Father!" she cried.

Nina jumped up. "Peter, bring the lantern." She opened the back door and stepped out onto the little wooden stoop. A gust of cold air swirled dry leaves across the kitchen floor.

"Is he alone?" Leah asked, and her voice trembled and broke. Was it from the sudden chill or from the expectation of what her father had discovered in Arkansas, Rachel wondered? She, too, waited breathlessly as the horse galloped around the corner of the house and was pulled to a stop. Was this how they had felt each time her father had returned from going in search of her? This time, would Jamie be with him, and would this mark a finish to the endless waiting the family had endured?

Peter stood behind her with the lantern held high. Slowly her father dismounted and turned to face his family waiting for word of Jamie. One look at his drawn and weary face gave Rachel the answer to their unspoken question. Her father looked old. How many more times could he set out on such a long and futile search that promised little hope of reward?

Nina stepped forward to lead him into the light and warmth of the house. "Welcome home, Tobias," she said softly. "Is there news of Jamie, any word of his whereabouts?"

"No, no word."

"There will be other times," Nina said. "We'll find him one day."

A strange look crossed his face, one almost of fear mixed with—what? In dread Rachel stared at him, caught by that expression of what looked to be—there was no other name for it—loathing. He looked at her and turned his face away into the shadows. Wearily he climbed the steps of the stoop.

"No," he said, his voice reverberating in the still night. "There will be no other times. We will never find Jamie."

"Father, why not?" Leah cried. "How can you say that?"

"Because this time I saw boys the age of Jamie who had been with the Indians even less time than he." The harshness of her father's voice filled Rachel with dread. Although he spoke the words to Leah, Rachel felt them directed at her. "*The boys were Indians,*" he said coldly. "They were Indians just as much as any boy born to the skin, heathens to the core. My son James John doesn't exist. I shall search for him no more."

9

"Milk or lemon?" Mrs. Penniman asked, smiling at Rachel over the china pot she held poised above the tea table. Rachel stared at the pot, hoping the correct answer would suddenly appear in the spiral of white steam that curled from the spout. If only Mrs. Penniman had asked one of the other women first.

Silence settled in the parlor as the others awaited her answer. Sixteen eyes fastened on her. Such a simple question—milk or lemon?

"Or perhaps you prefer your tea plain?" Mrs. Penniman asked.

"Yes, thank you, plain," Rachel responded, thankful for an easy solution to the problem.

"A little sugar then?" Mrs. Penniman continued, and Rachel wondered if the choices in this strange ritual of tea drinking would ever end.

"No, thank you, just plain," she said, holding fast to her first response. Mrs. Penniman poured the dark and steaming tea into the delicate cup decorated with a garland of miniature violets and roses around the rim. She handed the cup and a small linen napkin to Rachel who gripped the saucer with both hands. Conversation resumed as Mrs. Penniman repeated the ritual, passing a caravan of cups around the ring of seated women. The circle of eyes shifted away from Rachel.

She perched upright in her chair, afraid that any move on the stiff black horsehair that humped beneath her would send her sliding to the floor in a heap. She tried to draw a deep breath but felt bound by the tight sash encircling her waist. With each breath she felt the stiff bow press into the small of her back.

The sashes and Sunday shoes had been Nina's only concession to the importance of the occasion, and the three Porter women were dressed in their everyday, brown linsey-woolsey. But the others wore finely woven woolen dresses in shades of wild plum, the soft gray of a dove's belly or the green of the pine forests that fringed the ridges of *Paha Sapa,* the Black Hills, and crowned their rocky peaks.

Collars and cuffs of fine lace tatting or linen rested against their white necks and wrists. Mrs. Penniman herself wore a dress that whispered like a distant waterfall as she bent and straightened, pouring the brown liquid into cups and passing them one by one until each woman held one in the nest of her lap.

The tea was strong and tasted brackish, like water from a shallow woodland pool that seeps through moss and twigs. She should have asked for milk and two spoons of sugar as Leah had. The hot tea was making her perspire as well.

Mrs. Penniman's house, the largest and finest west of

the Mississippi Nina had said, was overly warm. The heat from the fire that burned in the hearth directly behind Rachel's chair made the air close and heavy, squeezing her lungs as tightly as the sash bound her ribs.

Such a house was beyond her imagining. The walls, covered with golden swirls, shimmered like Mrs. Penniman's dress, and seemed almost to move. And above, exactly centered in the room, hung a light such as she had never seen. From it cascaded prisms of glass that shimmered and blazed more brightly than the fingers of light within the crystal caves of *Paha Sapa*.

The light dazzled, the fire spread its warmth, the walls of the room swayed, closing around her until she felt faint and closed her eyes.

She must not lose consciousness. She would not shame Nina and Leah nor give these women a reason to laugh at her. Setting her lips in a stiff smile, she willed her lids to open. Eight pairs of eyes were turned on her once more.

"Don't you agree, Miss Porter?" Through a great cavern she heard the words and saw that they came from the girl in the dark green dress, a buxom girl with mousy hair, a very round face, and soft, plump hands. It wasn't until she repeated the question that Rachel realized it was directed at her. The cup clinked against the saucer in her lap and she gripped it tighter. She must answer, but what was it the girl had asked?

"Agree?" she forced herself to respond.

"Yes. Don't you agree that the Indians would be better off ?"

"Better off ?"

A look of impatience crossed the plump features. "Yes, better off if they would become Christians."

"Why should they wish to do that?" she asked in surprise. Remembrance of hard wooden prayer benches and narrow pews made her head ache.

"It is not a matter of *wish,* my dear," another voice said from the circle, the older woman in gray whose hair was almost white, Mrs. Penniman's mother. Little creases lined her face like the skin of windfall wild plums late in the season of falling leaves called autumn. Rachel tried to remember her name.

"Becoming Christian," the woman continued, "would surely make them more . . . well, more *civilized.* As it is, they remain heathens. And what can one expect of heathens except stealing and killing!"

Rachel's face flamed and angry words burned her throat even as she fought to swallow them. This time she must not speak too quickly. *Be like the fox,* she heard Waoka saying. *Use the power of what is in your head and do not speak what is in your heart until the anger has passed.* This time she would heed his voice. She must not forget she was a guest in this house. Her lips tightened to hold back the angry words that threatened to betray her.

"It must have been dreadful," the girl in plum said, breaking the sudden silence. She sat beside Leah and leaned toward Rachel expectantly. "It must have been just awful living in a tipi and being dirty all the time. I should hate not being able to bathe!"

"Whatever makes you think the Sioux don't bathe?" The sharp retort tumbled from her lips and eased the burning in her throat. "The Dakota are not *dirty*. We . . . they take great pride in keeping their bodies clean, free of dirt and vermin or disease. Our bodies are all that we truly possess, so it is only right to hold them in high esteem and to take great care. For the Sioux, that is law."

"What a strange notion!"

"Rachel knows lots of interesting things about the Sioux," Leah broke in, coming to her sister's defense. "In fact, she's writing a book about the years she lived with them. It's going to be a wonderful book full of all kinds of interesting stories."

Rachel's heart fluttered and plummeted in her chest.

"Indeed, Rachel? A book?" exclaimed Mrs. Penniman with a smile. "That's a very ambitious undertaking. We shall certainly all look forward to reading it."

Once again sixteen eyes turned to Rachel. Leah had only been trying to help. If only she hadn't spoken of the book to these women who would poke and pry and never understand.

"Not . . . not really a book. Just things I remember and hope not to forget—mostly things about what happened to me . . . what I learned from the Sioux. Things they hold to be true. . . ."

"What things?"

The eyes watched her expectantly. What could she tell them that would satisfy their curiosity but not cause the look she remembered so well on her father's face when he first saw her on the dock?

"Tell them about the circle, Rachel," Nina said softly.

They were watching her, waiting for her to speak, but

she could not talk about such sacred things to these people.

"Tell them the story about the circle," Nina suggested again, "the one you told Daniel yesterday at lessons."

"Perhaps," she said slowly, looking around the circle of curious women, a circle without *taku kapi,* a circle without meaning. Somehow she must try to make them understand.

"Yes, do tell us, Miss Porter!" the girl in the plum-colored dress urged.

Drawing a breath as deeply as she could, Rachel began cautiously, mindful of choosing each word with care. "The Sioux know that all things are connected," she said, drawing another breath, exhaling slowly. "The circle is *kapi*—it is the sign for . . . what stands for . . ." Forgetting the cup and saucer balanced in her lap, she raised her hands to form the shape of a circle in the air with her thumbs and forefingers. The word would not come.

"Symbol?" Nina prompted gently.

"Yes," she said smiling at Nina in gratitude as she grasped the saucer again before it could slide from her lap.

"The circle is the symbol that all things are one and must remain forever joined. The flowering tree within the closed hoop is the most sacred symbol, for the power of the world works in circles and the tree is the symbol of all living things."

She paused, aware of the faces watching her, waiting for her to continue. Behind her a log crackled and broke, sighing as it settled in the grate. She bent her head to listen to the voice of the fire. The words rose from the dying flames and hovered before her. One by one she plucked them as they gathered before her eyes, forming the pictures she knew so well.

"The circle is with us always." She spoke the words aloud. "The sky that curves above us is round, as is the earth, the mother of us all. The sun is round and the moon as well, and they come forth and go down again in a circle. The wind whirls and birds make nests in circles." As the images shifted, the words flowed faster.

"The tipis are round like the nests of birds, and they are always set in a circle, the tribe's larger hoop; for within the circle the spirit of Wakan-Tanka, the Power of the World, moves and all things are strong and safe. Even the seasons form a great circle in their changing and always return to where they began. And the life of a man is a circle. But when the circle is broken . . ." No words could tell of what might befall such bad *wakan*. The eyes watched her in silence, waiting.

"Tell them the story, Rachel, the one about the circle and the Sacred Pipe," Leah said, urging her to continue.

She could not. It was the most sacred story of the Dakota tribes, to be told only to those who would hold it true.

"Yes, tell us, Miss Porter," the girl in plum echoed. "We're dying to hear it!"

Across the circle, Rachel saw Nina's calm face and Leah's encouraging smile. She must not shame them. She struggled to make the words come. "There is a story . . ." she began. The voice of the fire died. The words faltered, drifted away to settle back among the embers. The women waited. *Picture Daniel,* a voice whispered in her head. *Tell the story to Daniel as you do every afternoon.* She looked down, away from the eyes that held her captive in this room, and gazed into the cup nestled in her lap. Daniel's small face floated on the surface of the half-filled cup of tea, smiling at her within the circle of the cup's rim. Tell *me* the story, the face seemed to say.

Her eyes held the face within the cup. *Forget the women. Look only into the cup. Tell the story to Daniel.* "There is a story," she began again, "about the Sacred Pipe of the Sioux nation, the pipe of red stone that is smoked in peace. It is our . . ." She caught herself. She must be careful. "It is their most sacred object, just as the story of the coming of the Pipe is sacred as well.

"It happened many years ago," she continued, speaking the words to Daniel. "One day, two Sioux hunters went out in search of game but had no luck. Late in the day they climbed a high hill and looked to the east, but still they saw nothing."

Gradually the words of the familiar story lifted her out of the room, carrying her farther and farther away until she stood on the hill with the two hunters. The wind-swept prairie stretched to the horizon. Only the grass stirred. Standing with the two hunters, she turned and looked into the setting sun.

"Far to the west, barely visible against the horizon, they saw something moving toward them. A beautiful woman, wearing a dress of white buckskin, was coming across the prairie carrying a bundle made of buffalo skin." As the woman approached, the words of the story fell away until only the beauty of the woman remained. The scene grew brighter, the woman spoke and Rachel heard her own voice say:

"'I have come to help your people,' the woman said to the hunters as she neared them, and when she spoke, her voice was like the mountain streams, for she was very sacred. 'Tell your chief to prepare a large tipi into which I will come to teach you sacred things.'

"The hunters returned to camp and told of the coming of White Buffalo Calf Maiden (for that was her name) to teach the people. They built a great tipi into which they all gathered, and when the beautiful maiden arrived, she entered the tipi and made a circle around the fire seven times.

"Then she spoke to the people gathered there, saying, 'I have made for you seven sacred circles that represent the seven ceremonies of the sacred pipe.'

"Out of the buffalo skin bundle she took the pipe and held it before them. 'This pipe,' she said, 'is *lela wakan*— very sacred.'

"Then she took the pipe of red stone and raised it skyward, saying, 'The bowl of the pipe is the sign of the circle of the earth in which all living things are as one. For a long time you will live under the shade of the sacred tree and your people will be united.'

"But before she disappeared she gave them a warning." Rachel's voice dropped almost to a whisper as she thought of the words the Buffalo Maiden had spoken.

"She said, 'A time will come when a dark storm will blow from the east and the tree shall die and the hoop crumble. But in time there will come two new circles. A new tree will grow stronger than before. At the end of this time, I will come again.' So promised White Buffalo Calf Maiden."

Dazzled by the wonder of the promise, Rachel lifted her eyes from the cup. Gazing straight before her, she looked directly into the accusing eyes of Mrs. Penniman's mother.

The beautiful maiden disappeared. The tipi collapsed. Rachel's voice faltered. Barely audible, she spoke the final words of the story with great effort.

"Thus the pipe of red stone and the circle are held sacred by the Sioux." The words stopped.

Her mouth was dry and she lifted the cup and took a drink. The tea was cold and bitter.

"Such an interesting story," Mrs. Penniman said, breaking the silence. "Don't you agree, Mother?"

"The part I liked best was where she tells them the tree will die and the hoop crumble. That should teach them a lesson they all deserve." The old woman's eyes bored into Rachel. "Don't you agree, Miss Porter, that the Indians should be taught a lesson?"

"A lesson?" Rachel struggled to keep her voice even, to hold back the feelings that threatened to erupt. "What kind of lesson?"

"They should be made to learn what it is like to be kidnapped and turned into slaves!"

"But Rachel wasn't a slave, Mrs. MacPherson!" Leah broke in as Rachel abruptly reached to set her cup and saucer on the table with a clatter. "She lived with a family."

"Well, a servant then, I'll warrant." The woman's voice touched the back of Rachel's neck with icy fingers as the dying fire surrendered to the cold north winds rising outside. "And heaven only knows what 'duties' she must have had to perform!"

"I was neither slave nor servant!" Rachel said fiercely. She could bear no more of this hateful woman. "I was taken in as a daughter, not a servant. They were my *family*, not my masters, and I only wish I were with them now!"

Silence fell on the room as the women stared in disbelief, their eyes reflecting amazement, horror, pain. She had spoken the unforgivable.

Rising without haste, Nina interceded once more. She extended her hand to Mrs. Penniman. "We must be on our way. It is growing late and I must stop at the dry-goods store before we start home. Thank you for your kind hospitality."

"Let me get your cloaks," Mrs. Penniman replied, rising as well. Rachel and Leah followed the two women out of the parlor and into the entrance hall where they collected their wraps. Behind them the inner room was silent.

"My mother means no harm, Rachel," Mrs. Penniman said as she handed Rachel her woolen cloak. "Do not be too hasty in judging her. Her brother, who would have been my uncle, was killed in a Shawnee uprising when she was just a child. She has never forgotten . . . nor forgiven." Rachel found herself without words.

As she stepped out into the darkening afternoon, a hand touched her shoulder. She turned back to look into Mrs. Penniman's troubled face framed in the light from the doorway. "I tried to warn you on the boat. It's going to be difficult for you at best, child. Don't make things harder on yourself than need be." Rachel could only nod.

Holding their cloaks tight around them against the sting of the winter wind, the three women huddled on the planked walk before the house. In the light from the windows, the distress in Nina's face was plain to read.

"I'm sorry, Nina," Rachel whispered. "I didn't intend to say those things, but I couldn't keep silent any longer. I know I have made it difficult for you."

"It is not myself that concerns me, Rachel. But we will talk about this later. Even for you I will not tell a lie. So now we must make some small purchase at the dry-goods store before it closes." She turned to cross the street with Leah at her side.

Rachel remained on the boardwalk, drawing a deep breath to clear the stuffiness that had made her head throb. She craved solitude, a luxury she had not been allowed since coming here two months ago.

Months. Already she was beginning to think like a white man. Already the image was fading. The wondrous passage of the moon's full circle, the visible power of Wakan-Tanka had dissolved into only a word, a *month*.

She needed to be alone. The kindness and concern of her sister and stepmother were more than she could bear right now, for the anger still rankled. She would never be at ease here, but the longer she remained the more she, like the circling moon's image, would begin to fade and dissolve—into what? Perhaps the obedient white daughter her father had dreamed of, only to be disappointed by the girl on the dock, the girl dressed in buckskin and tanned dark by the sun.

Across the street, Nina stopped and turned, waiting for her. Rachel hesitated, poised on the edge of the rough-sawn boards. Later she sometimes wondered which way she would have gone. Across the street to join Nina and Leah? Or would she have turned her back and run away, down the dark road toward home?

Before she could decide, a horse swung around the corner at the end of the street and galloped toward them. Even in the twilight Peter's upright figure was clearly discernible. The words he shouted carried on the wind.

"Mrs. Porter! Wait!" Like the steam rising from the horse's wet flank, Rachel's indecision evaporated in the cold air. She stepped into the street to meet him. The horse reared as Peter pulled him to a sudden stop before the three women. "Your husband said I might find you here. He sent me to fetch you."

"What is it, Peter?"

"It's the Jessups. They've come. He said to tell you they're at the house."

"Tell him we're on our way."

Rachel stood for a moment beside the blowing horse. The Jessups. The name formed on her lips. She tugged on Peter's stirrup. "Peter?" she asked. "The Jessups . . . ?"

"Yes, they've arrived, Rachel. Just a few moments ago from Jefferson City. Your Uncle Nathan and Aunt Sarah are home again."

Aunt Sarah had finally come! For more than two months Rachel had been alone, with no one who could understand her fears and longings. But now Aunt Sarah was home. Now Rachel would not be the only outcast, the only "squaw" and "heathen." Now there would be two of them. Tears stung her eyes but she blinked them away.

"Peter, let me have your horse." She gripped his boot and stirrup with both hands. "Please, Peter, let me ride your horse home now!" She had to get there right away, before Aunt Sarah could fade away.

"Ride my horse?" In the lowering darkness, Peter's voice revealed his astonishment.

"Rachel, you can't ride a horse in your dress," Nina said, voicing her disapproval.

"It's dark enough, no one will see. Please, Peter!" she tugged once more on his boot, resisting the urge to grab hold and pull him off his horse.

Slowly Peter slid from the horse and handed her the reins.

"For God's sake, Rachel, don't break your neck."

"Oh, Rachel, you'll just make Father angry again." Leah's voice floated to her from the darkness.

Grasping the horse's mane, Rachel lifted herself against his neck and threw her right leg across the back. For a moment the saddle upset her balance and the horse skittered beneath her, but she righted herself. Clutching the reins in her left hand and a fistful of mane in her right, she ignored the stirrups and pressed her knees hard into the horse's side.

"Aiyeee!" she cried in the familiar call of the braves setting out on the hunt. The horse responded and charged down the street at full gallop. The wind caught her hair, pulling it loose from the pins that had bound it in place, and lifted her skirts to swirl them about her knees.

"Aiyeee!" she called again through the darkness, as the cold air bit the tips of her fingers and her nose. How fine the cold wind felt after the heat of the stuffy parlor. How glorious the freedom after such a long confinement! If only this were Morning Star, her own horse. The mare would know to find her way, would carry Rachel home to the tipi that rose against the land somewhere far to the north.

Rachel gripped the horse's mane hard, swinging his head to the left as they turned and galloped together down the road leading to her father's house. This time Aunt Sarah would be waiting at the door.

Rachel lifted her head to catch the wind. Above her the moon began its slow rise, floating upward behind the black and twisted branches of distant oaks. Rachel looked and saw that the moon was full, an unbroken circle shining through the darkness to light the road that stretched ahead.

10

Aunt Sarah was not at the door to greet her. Instead, Rachel found her resting on the settle before the fire, still cold from the journey and shivering as though she would never be warm again.

But when Rachel burst through the door, Aunt Sarah reached out her arms to embrace her, crying, "Oh Rachel, how I have longed to see you! I have thought of you every day for the past seven years!"

Rachel scarcely recognized her aunt, now so thin and gaunt, her face flushed with fever instead of rosy from dancing as Rachel remembered her. Falling to her knees beside the settle, Rachel felt her aunt's arms wrap around her.

"I'm so glad you're here, Aunt Sarah!" she whispered. "I have felt so alone." She pressed her cheek against her aunt's breast. The faint scent of musk roses floated from the folds of her dress. "*Waun tiyata,*" Rachel murmured so softly the others could not hear. "*Waun tiyata.* Welcome home." For the first time since her return, Rachel felt she had indeed come home.

Looking up at her father, Rachel saw his eyes fixed

upon the two of them. His face, though, was expressionless, and she wondered if her father was happy to see Aunt Sarah again after so many years.

✳

In the first days of their return, before Uncle Nathan found a house for them and the family was all together, no one could help but notice Aunt Sarah's growing weakness. Her eyes were sunken in dark sockets as the strange fever consumed both her strength and her flesh. Often she lacked the strength to leave her bed, and Rachel and Leah took turns sitting beside her, wiping her hot forehead with cool, wet cloths. Nina cooked special dishes and coaxed Aunt Sarah to eat a few bites. Rachel saw the perpetual worried look that lined Uncle Nathan's face, and even her father showed concern, saying special prayers for Aunt Sarah every evening.

But within the second week of their coming, Uncle Nathan found a house for the two of them, and he and Aunt Sarah moved three miles across town.

"Let me go and help, please, Nina," Rachel begged. "I can walk there every day after chores."

"I think that's a fine idea, Rachel," Nina replied without hesitation. "The company will be good for your aunt as well as the help. And Leah can take on some of your chores here."

Her father agreed also, for it was only too clear that Aunt Sarah would need someone to help. "But not on Sunday," he added. "That is the Lord's Day and must be respected. Nathan will be at home on Sundays. He can make do for both of them."

The first morning Rachel arose early, eager to set out across town. By the time she arrived at the small frame house, Uncle Nathan was standing outside on the wooden stoop waiting for her. In the bright morning sun Rachel noticed how he, too, had changed. Since his and Aunt Sarah's return a week ago, she had not heard him laugh aloud. His brown hair was streaked with gray, and little gullies, like dry creekbeds, coursed his face.

"Your aunt's not well," he said, gazing past Rachel to the fields beyond the house as though hoping that some secret cure might spring to life among the brown blades of grass. "Dwelling on the past will only prolong her illness. We don't want to upset her by speaking of unpleasant things that are best forgotten."

He clasped her wrist and she felt the intensity of his words in the pressure of his fingers and saw his eyes reddened by sleepless nights. "You understand, don't you, Rachel?"

She could only nod. If she did not agree, he might not allow her to enter the house.

He released her wrist. "Good. Sarah is so looking forward to having you with her, I wouldn't want to disappoint her. We must do all we can to make her well again." His beard tickled her nose as he brushed his lips lightly against her forehead. "I know you'll take good care of her."

A rare smile lightened his eyes and softened the deep lines of his face. How her heart ached for the uncle she had known long ago, the gentle man who once had never been without a smile or a song on his lips.

She watched him walk down the narrow path to the road, broad shoulders hunched against the cold. An image shimmered in the morning light, a picture of Aunt Sarah dancing around the kitchen, skirts held high, boots tapping a quick beat on the wooden boards. Uncle Nathan had never walked by her without giving her a hug or wrapping his arms around her to kiss her full on the mouth—an act which always astounded Rachel who had never seen her father touch her mother in such a way. Sometimes Uncle Nathan had waltzed with Aunt Sarah in his arms, singing at the top of his lungs as they danced around the room with so much spirit that they set the china to rattling on the cupboard shelf.

But as Rachel opened the door, it was her uncle's warning, not sounds of laughter, that seemed to echo through the house.

*

Every day except Sunday, after her chores were done at home, Rachel set out across town. Through deep snow and cold that numbed her fingers and toes, she walked the three miles to Aunt Sarah's house, cleaned and cooked, shopped and mended, and felt happy to be doing it. She took care to cook dishes that might add flesh to her aunt's frail bones and color to her cheeks—rich rabbit stew; cornbread Nina had taught her to bake spread thick with fresh-churned butter; roasted apples with hickory nuts, windfalls that Daniel had gathered long before the last of autumn's leaves had fallen.

Within a few days of their move and Rachel's coming, Aunt Sarah's fever began to abate just as mysteriously as it had appeared, and the following morning she was up and dressed by the time Rachel arrived. As she gradually regained her strength, Aunt Sarah began to help with the dusting or set the next day's bread to rise as Rachel prepared the evening meal. Then the two of them talked quietly as they waited for Uncle Nathan to return home from work.

"How was it for you, Rachel?" Aunt Sarah asked one afternoon not long after she was up and about. She stood with Rachel at the sink drying pewterware as Rachel finished scouring and rinsing it. "Was it very difficult for you those years with the Sioux?"

The question startled Rachel. No one else had ever asked her about that time away. No doubt her father had instructed the others not to ask such questions just as Uncle Nathan had instructed her. His warning echoed in her mind, and she shivered at the remembrance of his cold fingers on her wrist.

"Uncle Nathan said talk of such things would upset you, Aunt Sarah. He told me never to mention it."

"Nonsense." The woman's face tightened and for a moment the towel hung motionless. "What will make me ill again is not knowing. You can't know how I have worried about you all these years because I never knew what was happening to you. You are the only one who can ease my mind."

Rachel's thoughts struggled back to the time that seemed always to hover beneath some distant horizon. "It was hard in the beginning," she said slowly. "When they took me away from you and Jamie, it was very hard.

And the journey north. . . ." She had never spoken of that journey, not even to Tanka and Ina. And as time passed the memories had dimmed, growing fainter each year like an echo fading in the distance.

"I lived with a family of the Teton tribe." She handed the last of the pewter plates to her aunt. "The brave who captured me sold me to a chief, Waoka, who became my Dakota father. He paid many horses to save me from that *wicasa sica,* to make that man let me go, and he drove him away from the camp. Later, when I knew the language and could understand, Waoka told me that the Indians who attacked us were a band of renegade Sioux, braves who had been banished from their tribe for breaking tribal laws. After their tribe sent them away, they headed south. They weren't looking for us at all. It was only food and horses they wanted."

Sudden understanding crossed Aunt Sarah's face. "And by that time, of course, our horses weren't at the fort and our food was almost gone."

"I don't remember that day very well."

"On the day of the attack, all the men, and the horses too, were out in the fields planting crops. All except Peter. He was standing guard that day."

"I do remember that he went out to meet the Indians. I was sure they would kill him."

"We all thought so," Aunt Sarah said. "He was very brave. We thought the Indians were a war party because they were painted. I never did understand why they didn't kill us all."

"Waoka said that when they couldn't find horses, they took the three of us to trade. He gave the brave four beautiful horses for me." *Hoksiyopa*, was all Waoka had said as he stroked her hair with his fingertips, but she had known from his voice and his gentle touch that she was to be loved and cared for. "After he drove the brave away, he took me to live with his family." The memory stirred her heart with longing.

"Did they treat you well?"

"They made me part of their family. They were very kind to me."

"Kind?" Her aunt's brows drew together and her dark eyes widened as she gazed past Rachel into the fire as though searching the flames for an answer. "I would not have thought such a thing possible. But I thank God for that, Rachel. Every day I prayed that you were not suffering also. Sometimes I think it was the thought of you that kept me alive. I had to live to know if you were safe."

Tears filled Sarah's eyes and she turned her head away, stooping to place another log on the fire.

"Oh Aunt Sarah," Rachel cried in dismay. "You mustn't think such things. I'm afraid you might get sick again. Uncle Nathan was right. I think I've only made you feel worse."

Aunt Sarah stood erect, her eyes still moist. "Of course you haven't, child. I'm only thankful that you were spared, but sometimes my emotions get the better of me." She smiled at Rachel through the tears. "You see? I'm just being foolish. You mustn't worry. Nathan knows how happy I am to have you with me for these few hours each day." She reached for Rachel's hand and stroked the rough skin with fingertips that brushed across the reddened knuckles. "But what about you, my pet?" she asked, smiling again at Rachel. "Are you happy now?"

Rachel's determination not to cause her aunt any pain dissolved.

"Oh, Aunt Sarah," she cried, and for the first time since her return, the tears ran down her cheeks unchecked. "I didn't *want* to come back. Waoka and Ina are not the parents who bore me, but I miss them so. I long to be back with them, and I cannot hide my longing from Father. He knows I am not happy here, and he hates me for it."

"Oh, no, child! It isn't *you* he hates. Most likely he can't understand how you could have grown to love them, the very people he *has* hated for so long. It must hurt him to know they have replaced him in your heart."

"I didn't mean for it to be so! In the beginning I thought—I prayed—he would come and take me home again. But as each day passed and we traveled farther north, I began to despair of ever being found. I couldn't bear to believe they were all still alive and together while that brave was taking me farther and farther away!"

Rachel shuddered and closed her eyes to shut out the nightmare. But the dark face with its jutting, hawklike nose loomed over her while beyond the fire the other faces floated, watchful and gleaming in the firelight. The brave's hard body shoved her down against the earth while his breath, reeking with whiskey from the fort, washed across her face and made her retch.

"Oh Aunt Sarah!" Her voice was no more than a whisper. "He did terrible things to me!" She covered her eyes with her hands, wanting the darkness to cover his face as he tore at her clothes, the weight of his body pressing on hers. "I couldn't bear it! I hoped I would die!" Sobs shook her as Aunt Sarah's arms folded around her.

"Oh, my poor child! And only ten! How terrible for you! How could you have endured? My poor baby, how well I understand. Of course you wanted to die!"

Rachel sobbed until the tears washed the darkness from her mind. Slowly the sobs diminished and she heard the soft murmur of her aunt's voice.

"There now. My poor child. Hush now. It's over. We're safe now." Aunt Sarah's arms still held her.

Rachel drew a deep breath. From somewhere deep inside her, thoughts emerged she had never known before.

"When no one came," she said, and her voice trembled only a little, "when I thought, even wished, that I would die, it was easier to believe that all of them were dead—Father, Mother, Leah, and Jamie, even myself, Rachel Porter. I left them all behind me somewhere on that trail leading north. They disappeared almost as though they had never been."

"Yes, you were so young then, I can see how that could be." Aunt Sarah smoothed back a lock of hair from Rachel's forehead. "Your Indian family must have thought you were a gift from the heavens, such a lovely young white-skinned girl with hair the color of the setting sun and eyes like an autumn sky. Who could help but love you?"

"Sometimes I feel my father does not."

"You mustn't think that, Rachel. I know he loves you

very much. But it's not in his nature to show his love easily."

Rachel went to the window and pressed her cheek against the frosted glass. The chill of it steadied her. Outside, winter's early dusk crouched in wait of the setting sun. A midwinter freeze had settled over the land. "I think he cannot forgive me for having been one of them," she said quietly. "I have seen the way he watches me, and sometimes I wonder if there's something terribly wrong with me."

"Whatever would make you think such a thing?"

"I know how Father must have dreamed of finding his lost daughter again. But I am not that daughter. He wants only Rachel, not Kata Wi. And I cannot cut her out of my heart for all his wishing."

"Of course you can't." Her aunt came to stand behind her at the window. "Perhaps in time your father will grow to love Kata Wi as well as Rachel. But you must understand, he has good reason to hate the Indians. You must be patient with him."

Against the darkening landscape a few flakes of snow began to fall, each separate crystal swirling in lazy spirals to the ground where it disappeared in drifts already fallen.

"What I fear, Aunt Sarah," Rachel said, her voice still a whisper, "is that now Father cannot love even the part of me that is Rachel. Sometimes he looks at me as though . . . I cannot find the words. It is a look that freezes my heart and takes my breath away. I think it is because of me that Father will no longer search for Jamie."

"How could that be?"

"Because although I have come home again, he still believes he has lost his daughter. I think he can't bear to lose his son in the same way. It is easier for him to believe Jamie is dead."

"Oh, Rachel, I only pray you're wrong."

"I fear some evil *wakan* has found its way into my heart. It has followed me down the river and lives with me in my father's house. And I wonder if I'll ever grow to love this man who seems almost to wish me gone again."

For a few moments her aunt did not reply.

"Your father doesn't wish you gone, Rachel." Aunt Sarah's voice was tremulous as though Rachel's fear had crept into her own heart. "It's those years you were gone that trouble him, for he's not part of them. He must wonder what it was like for you, how you lived, who you were with, whom you came to love and who loved you. And yet he can't bear to ask or to know for fear his knowing will shut a door that can't be opened again. The greatest pity, though, is that by not knowing he shuts the door himself."

Rachel heard the sadness in her aunt's voice and felt it was for all of them, but perhaps most of all for Uncle Nathan who wished never to speak of what had happened.

The brief flurry of snow was over, and already a few random stars gleamed in the indigo sky. Behind her Aunt Sarah suddenly trembled.

"You're shivering, Aunt Sarah!" Contrite at having ignored how tired and cold her aunt must be after a long day, she took the shawl from the settle, wrapped it around her aunt's thin shoulders. Kneeling on the hearth, she pumped the fire with the bellows until the flames leaped high. "Uncle Nathan will scold me for certain."

"He can't scold us if he doesn't know. And we shan't tell him for it would only trouble him."

Rachel took her aunt's hand. It was icy and she rubbed it gently between her two palms. "I couldn't bear it if Uncle Nathan didn't let me come again."

"Your uncle is a good man, Rachel, and he means only to do what is right. But he also can't bring himself to speak of those things. You see, when he first asked me, I thought he wanted to know the truth, but I should have kept silent." She glanced through the window at the oncoming night. "He'll soon be home and you must go, too." She kissed Rachel on the cheek. "Hurry now. It's already dark and you must get home or it will be Nina and your father who scold."

"I'll be back tomorrow. Nobody will keep me from coming here, Aunt Sarah, as long as you want me!" Rachel pulled on the boots she had left by the door, laced them up, and wrapped her cloak around her. The sharp wind caught the door as she opened it, almost pulling it from her hand.

"You're always welcome here, Rachel. I hope you never doubt that. I don't know what I'd do without you." Aunt Sarah pressed her cheek to Rachel's. Her skin was soft and dry like the dust that blows across the autumn prairie.

Halfway down the path, Rachel turned to wave. The figure silhouetted in the doorway looked so frail and wan that the sight made her breath catch in her throat. "Keep warm, Aunt Sarah!" she called and waved again. A thin arm lifted in return as the door closed, shutting in the light. Evening was melting into night, and the pathway home would be hard to follow. Holding her cloak more closely around her, Rachel turned and hurried through the snow.

*

That night, during prayers, kneeling on the rough boards before the fire, Rachel wondered for the first time if Aunt Sarah had been happy to return home to Uncle Nathan or if she, too, had found another to love. It was a question she had never considered, had perhaps not wanted to ask, wishing to keep whole her own past memories of her aunt. Was it surprising, then, that others should do the same with her? Only Daniel had begged Rachel to tell him about her life as an Indian, and only he had no vision of the younger Rachel, no memories to hold unchanged.

Today, after so many years, she had spoken about herself and had found it strangely healing. Perhaps Aunt Sarah too would find it healing. And what had she told Uncle Nathan? What was the "truth" he couldn't speak of, the events that had altered the path of their lives? Tomorrow, in spite of Uncle Nathan's protests, she would ask.

11

The next day, as she went about her work, Rachel looked forward to the end of afternoon when she and Aunt Sarah could talk quietly together by the fire. A good scrubbing for the kitchen floor was her final task. Then she could sit beside her aunt on the settle and converse until it was time for Uncle Nathan to arrive home.

At midafternoon she knelt in the narrow passageway that led to the small bedroom beyond and began to scrub the wide pine boards of the floor with a brush and bucket of soapy water. Her arms began to burn from the lye soap Nina had taught her to make only a few weeks earlier.

But before she had made her way across even half of the planked floor, Uncle Nathan suddenly appeared at the door with a freshly cut spruce tree slung over his shoulder. Rachel looked up in surprise at the tree with branches so wide it could barely pass through the door.

"Surely you haven't forgotten about Christmas?" he said to them in mock alarm as Aunt Sarah rose from the settle to greet him. "That will never do! It's only five days away and we have nothing to show for it!"

Delight and amazement washed Aunt Sarah's pale cheeks with a sudden flush of color. "Oh, Nathan, how lovely! I had almost forgotten. How good of you to remember." She rose on tiptoe to kiss him on the lips, but ever so slightly his head turned and the kiss fell on the side of his chin. Bending his head to return his wife's greeting, his lips grazed her forehead. Just as he greeted me my first morning here, Rachel thought, and wondered what had happened to the joyous dancing man who had once hugged and kissed Aunt Sarah without restraint.

"It's a beautiful tree, Nathan," Aunt Sarah said, but the luster of her smile had dimmed. Pain shadowed her eyes and she turned her face away. "Where did you find it?"

"In the woods just east of town. I looked for the finest pine tree in the forest. This was it," he said proudly. He set the tree in the corner and a light dusting of snow fell from the branches.

"It's a fine tree, Nathan," Aunt Sarah said softly. She stood behind him, her frail fingers resting on the sleeve of his coat. "We'll move the table and stand the tree right in the center of the room."

"I hoped you would be pleased." He turned to smile at her. The smile spoke both love and sadness and allowed Rachel a brief glimmer of the uncle she had once known. Her heart ached for these two who seemed so full of love and yet so distant, separated by the strange turn of events that had reshaped their lives.

"I'll build a stand for it tomorrow," he said.

"And Rachel and I will pop some corn to string on the branches, and perhaps some berries if the birds haven't found them all. It will be like old times, won't it, Nathan?" Aunt Sarah's eyes were soft and pleading.

"Like old times," he echoed, but his voice was hollow. He hung his jacket on a nail beside the door and crossed to the fire where he stood with outstretched hands, his back to the room. Silence stood awkwardly in their midst.

Hastily Rachel finished scrubbing the floor and with only a brief good-bye set out for home before the sun had touched the western horizon where earth and sky became one.

*

"They called me 'squaw,' Aunt Sarah," Rachel said the following afternoon as they strung kernels of popped corn with needles and coarse black thread. She had searched for berries, but what few the birds hadn't eaten had long since withered on the bushes.

"On the boat coming down river, some of the men, and women, too, they called me 'squaw.'"

"I know. I've been called that as well, and probably a lot worse." Aunt Sarah stood at the kitchen table kneading a Christmas stollen.

Earlier that morning Peter had stopped by with a small packet of candied citron and lemon peel. "In return for a thick slice of stollen," he said, "and just to make sure that Rachel hadn't disappeared again. I never see you anymore," he added, turning to her with a frown. Rachel blushed at her aunt's sudden glance and at the knowledge that since Aunt Sarah's and Uncle Nathan's return, she had missed Peter's company. With Aunt Sarah's promise that he would have the first piece, Peter left again, promising to return to claim his reward.

"Those people have little better to occupy their time but to think poorly of others," Aunt Sarah continued now as she sprinkled the precious bits of peel on top of the lightly floured dough and pressed into it with the heels of her hands, rolling it over and over until it was smooth and pliable. "They call themselves Christian but show little charity to any but their own selves. You must pay those people little mind." Her voice held a sharp edge that Rachel had never heard before.

"How was it for you, Aunt Sarah?" she asked timidly, her voice barely audible above the sound of crackling logs. "When they found you . . . did you wish to come back?" For a moment she feared her aunt might not answer as she carefully divided the dough and set each portion into a greased and floured pan.

"You know, Rachel," Aunt Sarah said at last, and a faint smile lifted the corners of her mouth, "it's strange, but no one else has ever asked me that." Covering the pans with two damp cloths, she set them near the hearth to rise. For a moment she stood silent again, peering into the fire as though searching for the answer. "I was sold to the Comanche—to a brave who needed a . . . a wife." She spat the word as though it left a bitter taste in her mouth. Never before had Rachel heard her aunt speak with such vehemence, and she dreaded her next words.

"He took me to live with him as a slave," she continued, but now her voice was so low Rachel had to bend close to hear, "to do with as he wished. When I fought him, he beat me, so I learned to do his bidding." Her hands trembled and Rachel reached and held one. Fine blue lines traversed the cold fingers. "Often I thought of ending my life, but he never let me out of his sight. When he went hunting, he tied me to a *tipi* pole. I never found a way."

Rachel's mind recoiled from the thought, but Aunt Sarah's voice was matter-of-fact, as though this were an idea she had grown accustomed to.

"Then I discovered I was carrying a baby. After that I no longer thought about killing myself."

"A baby? Oh, Aunt Sarah!" Rachel cried, overcome with a feeling of helplessness. What could she say to this woman who had endured more than she could ever imagine? She had been saved from such a fate, but no kind father had suddenly appeared to rescue Aunt Sarah.

"A little girl. I named her Tautaijah, Prairie Flower." She looked at Rachel through tear-filled eyes. "You had a little cousin, a beautiful baby girl. She died when she was only two. After that it didn't seem to matter whether I lived or died." The voice was low, without expression. She spoke of these things as though they had happened to someone in another lifetime.

"I lived with the Comanche for almost seven years before I was found. The Comanche were not like the Sioux. I was glad to leave them. But most of all I was thankful to be free of the brave who took me." She fell silent. After a moment she continued, but her voice shook and the words were hesitant.

"But I—I, too, have found it difficult to come back. And it hasn't been easy for your Uncle Nathan. It never is. It's important for you to understand that. You know, of course, that he and I have never been able to have a child. That's what he can't speak of now. The baby. I should never have told him." She gripped Rachel's hand with unexpected force and her eyes grew dark with some secret knowledge.

"Oh, Rachel, don't ever tell him we have talked of this. He would grow to hate me. This is very hard for me to say to you, you are still so very young, but it's important that you know. Since my return, he hasn't . . . Nathan can't . . . he hasn't lain with me as a husband. Oh, he shares my bed, for he would never be so unkind as to shame me, but he can't bring himself to—to love me in the way a husband should. Even if I weren't ailing . . ." Her voice trailed off. "But perhaps it is just as well . . ."

Rachel wanted to cry out that Uncle Nathan *was* unkind. How could he not love Aunt Sarah as his wife after all she had suffered? Perhaps in some strange way her illness was connected to that lonely bed, to his nightly greeting with lips that barely touched Aunt Sarah's upturned forehead.

As though reading her thoughts, her aunt gripped both her hands and gazed hard into her eyes. "You mustn't think less of your uncle, Rachel. He's not to blame. Don't fault him for what he can't help. It's not easy for any of us. You must try to understand or it will be hard for you."

Mrs. Penniman had spoken almost those same words

to her that afternoon at her house. What was it they both foresaw for her? Her heart cried out to be gone from this place that had entrapped her like some wild animal caught in a hunter's snare.

And how long might it be before the strange illness that wracked her aunt attacked her, too, bringing the fever that would consume her spirit as well as her flesh?

Shuddering, she drew a deep breath and inhaled the pungent aroma of fresh pine. The familiar odor stabbed her heart. Now, in the season of deep snows, the tribe would have moved to higher ground. They'd be camped somewhere in the foothills of *Paha Sapa* or perhaps the Big Horn Mountains, the tipis nestling in the pines on the eastern slopes, protected from the western gales that whipped across the mountaintops. Her family would be clustered around the fire in their tipi, just as she and Aunt Sarah stood together in this room, safe from winter winds.

Perhaps even now Ina and Tanka were sewing soft doeskin into moccasins for the coming spring. Waoka would be close by, shaping new arrows out of dried willow branches. And White Hawk—what would he be doing in this time of early dusk? He was seldom still, always in motion like the bird that was his namesake. Lithe and sure-footed, he could leap onto his stallion's back on the run and lean so low over the withers that he became one with the horse. But he could be as gentle as he was strong and was skilled at mending the wing of a fallen bird or setting a rabbit's broken leg. Once he had found her in tears because of a fox cub whose leg had been cruelly twisted in a snare. He had teased her about her tears, for Dakota children seldom cry, but he had put his arm around her shoulders to comfort her and then healed the cub's wounded leg before setting it loose again.

It was in these dying days, when darkness came early to swallow the winter light, that the tribe renewed the lessons of earth and sky. There would be stories: winter was the time for telling. Perhaps even now an elder told the story of the child with flaming hair, the white girl who had stayed with the Dakota for seven years and left a woman.

Or perhaps her story had already been forgotten. Perhaps by now only the wind carried it. In the kitchen, Rachel bent her head to listen to the wind blowing fiercely against the walls of the house.

12

Christmas came and went with little cele-
bration, the occasion marked only by a
lengthy church service and a sermon that dwelt on the
solemnity of baby Jesus's birth, the infant who became
the white man's savior.

Only Aunt Sarah's and Uncle Nathan's pine tree with
its festoons of popped corn seemed festive to Rachel.
Although her father had stated the tree was nothing but
a pagan ritual and had scarce to do with the holy day of
birth, Rachel took great pleasure in it. Each breath she
drew spoke of the presence of Wakan-Tanka and the
sacred circle of life.

Not long after Christmas the great snows swept across
the prairie from the west, carving deep drifts in front of
doors and windows, filling the paths and streets, making
travel difficult. With each new layer of snow, Rachel
found the route to Aunt Sarah's house took her longer
to walk each day. Then, toward the middle of January,
another blizzard swept down from the north bringing
more snow and icy winds.

Rachel awoke the morning after the great blizzard to

the sight of clear blue skies above a bright sun and a mountain of dazzling snow that reached the eaves of the shed out back and blotted out the pathway they had kept shoveled. In the distance the road to town had disappeared.

"We'll have to wait here until the breaking out," Nina said to her as they washed the breakfast dishes. "Your father almost couldn't get to the shed to feed the animals. There'll be no way to get to town until the wagons with the plows arrive to clear the road. But Sarah will be in good hands. Nathan will be at home."

Rachel thought it was just as well. Her throat hurt when she swallowed, and although her skin felt warm to touch, she shivered and wrapped an extra shawl around her shoulders.

Leah and Daniel were happy that the snow would keep Rachel home with them for a few days. "We never see you anymore!" They both echoed Peter's words.

At midday, all except Rachel bundled into boots, scarves, mittens, and extra jackets to clear a path to the pump and the shed while their father chopped firewood to rebuild the depleted pile under the lean-to outside the back door.

"You're to stay in by the fire, Rachel," Nina ordered after she had noticed her flushed cheeks and placed cool fingers against her warm forehead. "We can't have you getting sick, too."

It was useless to argue with Nina's firm voice, and secretly she was glad to be able to sit by the fire and have time to herself, time to write her remembrances of those seven years she hoped never to forget. She gathered her exercise book, a pen, and bottle of ink, and sat at the end of the table nearest the fire. The sun on the snow filled the room with light.

Page by page the lesson books were beginning to fill. At first the struggle to write so many thoughts had seemed overwhelming, but she had persevered and every day the writing progressed.

Before the arrival of Aunt Sarah and Uncle Nathan she had written at the kitchen table when her father was away from the house. But lately she had done much of the writing at Aunt Sarah's house after chores were done, while supper was simmering over the fire. On days when Aunt Sarah felt well enough, she often sat across from Rachel, encouraging her to tell about Waoka, Ina, White Hawk, and Tanka, about the tribe, where she had traveled, what she had seen.

What next to tell about and how best to tell it were the questions that arose each time Rachel sat down with pen and exercise book before her. But soon she had discovered that telling Aunt Sarah made the writing come easier, the words less halting.

Pulling the shawl more tightly around her, she opened the exercise book that was already filled and read the first words she had written. Letters were uneven, many words were misspelled, but she had worked hard, had persisted, and now what she had written filled her with pride. It was her story, to share or not as she saw fit. The book was a companion that would be with her for as long as she wished. She had only to open the cover for this friend to suddenly appear.

In the warm light of the afternoon sun she began to

read, and the words curled around her, shutting out the rest of the world.

*

Begun this tenth day of December (the *Moon of Frost in the Tipi*), in the year 1845, in the town called St. Joseph sitting midway on the Missouri River.

Peter had told her that. She hoped he was correct.

I write this at the table in my father's house, having been brought back here after living seven summers with the Dakota far to the north. Of the journey north I shall say little, except that it was a hard time full of sadness. This book will speak only of what is most important to me and what I wish never to forget: my Dakota family, the tribe and how it was to live as part of the great Sioux nation.

First I shall speak of the tribe, for the Dakota are like the prairie, never still, always moving. We never stayed in one place for long or planted crops, and until the season of great snows came we followed the buffalo herds, roaming far across the northern plains. We stayed in camp until the herd was gone. Then we moved on.

Whenever our tribe moved, it was the task of Tanka and me to carry our tipi and put it up again when we stopped. Our tipi was great in size because my father was chief. It held five of us with comfort and space for all. It had five supporting poles, twelve for framing, and sometimes we used as many as thirty skins to cover it, carefully tanned by Ina, Tanka, and me.

It is not easy to build a good tipi. The frame must not

form a true cone but must tilt slightly to give more space for standing up in the rear and to permit smoke to rise more easily through the smokehole.

The tipi is important to the tribes, and I shall speak more of it later. Tanka and I were the best tipi builders in our tribe. Waoka often said so.

*

Rachel paused and looked once more at the beginning. These first words she had struggled over sounded strange, as if someone else had written them. How much easier the words came now, how much more like her own voice they sounded. She turned the pages slowly, her eyes skimming the entries she had made, and noticed with pride how her writing had improved as she progressed. She glanced at a few of the more recent pages.

December 14 Today the doctor came to see my aunt who is very ill. I wish Wawokiye could come to her. He is *Wicasa-Wakan*, our holy man who heals and our prophet.

No one in the tribe has greater power than *Wicasa-Wakan*, not even my father, the Chief. I know he could heal Aunt Sarah . . .

December 18 I like to hear Daniel laugh, so I tell him things I know he'll find funny, like what the Dakota eat: cactus buttons, rose berries, willow buds, buffalo berries, birds' eggs, and fish caught with hooks made from the ribs of mice. Daniel wants to make a fishhook from a mouse when summer comes. He laughed when I told him about our mud battles. Because the tribes often camp beside a river or creek, all Sioux children learn to swim and love to play water games. We have battles by placing small balls of wet mud on the tips of long willow sticks. Then we bend them and let them go. The mud balls fly through the air! Daniel wants to try that, too.

Sometimes I forget about Father's order and then I tell Daniel about my other family. I have told him about White Hawk and Tanka, about playing together on the frozen streams in winter, sliding on the ice in much the same way that people here go sledding or skating. Often Tanka and I would sit on a deerskin while White Hawk pulled us across the ice. Sometimes, if the wind had blown when the water was freezing, the ride would be very bumpy. Once we hit the end of a log that had frozen just under the surface of the water. We tipped over, pulling White Hawk down with us, and the three of us laughed until our sides ached.

December 27 Today Nina and Leah have gone to a quilting bee. Although I would be interested to see one sometime, I did not go because of coming to Aunt Sarah's house. From the way Nina describes a quilting bee, it sounds like preparing for a new tipi.

When it was time for us to make a new tipi, we invited all the women of our tribe to a feast of roasted buffalo meat and pemmican. Afterward, the women helped with the cutting and sewing of the hides. There was always much gossip and storytelling which made the work easier and the time pass quickly.

Tanka and I always placed the front of the tipi to face the sunrise which helps to brace it against the west winds on its back. When tipis are new they are white as snow but soon they darken from the wind and rain and often the top becomes black from wood smoke. You can almost see through a tipi after it has been used a long time. Nothing is more beautiful than a circle of tipis glowing in the darkness of night from the fires burning within.

It is important to build good tipis. I have written much about them because they are the center of the family and of the tribe as well . . .

*

Outside, voices called back and forth as the others dug their way through drifts of snow. It was a cheerful sound in the quiet afternoon. Rachel turned a few more pages, pausing to read the story she had told Daniel on the first day of the new year.

January 2 (the *Moon of Popping Trees*) Yesterday, I told a story to Daniel that he enjoyed. I shall write it here so it won't be forgotten. There is so little opportunity for telling stories in our father's house. This is the story just as I told it to Daniel.

Many winters ago in the land of *Paha Sapa*, there lived two small boys. One day, when no one was watching them, they decided to go on a hunting trip of their own. They wanted to find out what the rest of the world was like. All day they walked, looking at the country and eating much wild fruit along the way. The shadows began to lengthen, and the two boys discovered they were far from home. They had never been away from the tipi before. Night was falling and the boys were afraid.

When they saw that they were being followed by *Mato*, the Bear, their fear grew and they turned and ran just as fast as they could. The bear also ran fast and drew closer. He snarled and growled and the boys knew he would soon be upon them.

Full of fear the boys cried out to Wakan-Tanka to help them. They fell to the ground, hoping the bear might pass over them. Then they felt a trembling beneath them. They raised their heads to see if the bear was shaking them. No, the ground around them was rising towards the sky. They were on top of a mountain of solid rock, safe from the jaws of the great bear below.

In his efforts to reach them, the bear's claws tore great jagged gashes in the sides of the rock. To this day Devil's Tower stands near *Paha Sapa*. Its scarred sides and flat top will always be a reminder of the kindness of Wakan-Tanka and his watchfulness over all Sioux children.

But now and then the mighty Thunder Bird comes to the top of Devil's Tower. There he beats his mighty drums, causing the sounds of thunder and the great storms that follow.

Rachel set aside the first exercise book and picked up the one she had started only the week before, turning to the page she had filled most recently. It was the day Mrs. Penniman had come by to give Nina a jar of apple butter and one of sweet pickles, a gift to honor the coming of the Three Wise Men.

*

January 6 Mrs. Penniman has just left after bringing us what she called a Twelfth Night gift. She left shortly after I returned home from Aunt Sarah's. Nina said she "stayed to tea," so I'm glad I wasn't there. It makes me think of the afternoon we went to her house. Nina says it's "coming to call" and that I shall do it, too, after I am married someday. What a strange thought! The Sioux "come to call" as well and they also have rules. The rules are important for me to remember in case I should one day return. I dream of that more often lately.

If the flap of a tipi is open, a friend may enter directly. But if it's closed, he must announce his presence and wait until he's invited in.

When a man visitor enters the tipi, he goes to the right and waits for the owner to invite him to sit in the guest's place to the left of the owner at the back of the tipi (where it is tallest). A woman enters after the man and goes to the left.

No visitor should ever walk between the fire and another person but should pass behind whoever is seated.

Women must never sit cross-legged like men. They can sit on their heels or with their legs to one side.

When invited to a feast, guests must bring their own bowls and spoons and must eat all they are given.

Only the elders can begin a conversation. The younger ones must remain silent unless they are invited to speak by an elder. (This rule gave me much trouble!)

When the owner of the tipi cleans his pipe everyone should leave.

I had difficulty at first remembering these rules. Now

I must start all over again learning the rules of "coming to call" at houses.

*

Rachel turned to a fresh page and dipped her pen into the ink, carefully writing the day's date. Line by line she began to fill the next page.

January 15 Today we are snowed in and must wait at home until the "breaking out." Nina says that is when they gather together many wagons drawn by strong horses. Each wagon pulls a heavy board that scrapes the snow off the road as the wagons pass by. I have not yet seen such a thing. Leah is excited. She says all the horses and wagons come from miles around to clear the snow. When all the roads have been cleared, everyone gathers in the center of town for hot cider and games of fox and geese or snowball fights.

The Indians play these games as well, but when the snow gets very deep in the mountains, they stay by the fires inside the tipis. When Tanka and I were younger, our mother used this time to teach us how to polish quills and sew beautiful designs with them, or how to fashion a pair of moccasins or hide boots that would keep our feet snug and dry. We often laughed together at our clumsiness, but Ina never lost patience and showed us again how to do it properly when we made mistakes.

Now she and Tanka will be sewing many fine garments, for it has already been arranged for Tanka to be married in the spring. There will be great festivities because she is the daughter of the Chief Who Rules the

Tribe and she will marry the son of the Chief Who Fights the Wars. She has known him from the day of her birth and is very happy to be marrying such a fine man. Oh, how I wish I could be there on her marriage day!

Today I could not go to Aunt Sarah's because of the snow and because now I am feeling feverish.

Through the window I can see long icicles hanging from the roof. They touch the tops of the snowdrifts. In the bright sun they gleam like crystal. They call to my mind the crystal caves of *Paha Sapa* and the time I was taken there by Waoka for the healing waters that flow from the rocks. It is a memory I shall cherish forever.

At *Paha Sapa* great needles of rock reach up to touch the sky. The buffalo cannot range the sacred slopes, but the hills abound with elk, antelope, and small mountain goats that run up and down the rocky mountainsides. On sunny days great billowing clouds are shadows moving on the plains like water, dividing light and dark; and far below, the highland meadows stretch to the horizon, fields of sweet clover, flax, stonecrop and buckwheat. On dark days the voice of Thunder Bird calls across the rocky slopes, and late at night the rocks turn into spirits that sing strange songs, awakening the echoes.

The most sacred tipi poles are cut from the forests of *Paha Sapa*, and deep within the sacred hills wondrous things occur. Far below the mountain peaks, within the caves of crystal and gold, great mysteries unfold. No one who has not been there can know. I can only try to tell about it for my words can't describe this strange and marvelous time. What follows is just as I remember.

One winter day, when we were camped in the foothills,

I slipped and cut my leg on a jagged rock. The cut was both deep and long, and although Ina dressed it with a poultice of yarrow root and gave me tea brewed of wild garlic, the wound did not heal. I was in much pain, and when fever set in Waoka sent for Wawokiye who said he had been expecting the summons for only the night before he had dreamed of the crystal cave. He told Waoka he would take me to the cave and leave me alone there for two days and two nights. Then I would be healed.

At first I was frightened at the thought of being alone in a dark cave, but by the time we set out with Wawokiye and Waoka pulling me up the mountain on a travois, the pain was so fierce and the fever so burning I had no clear thoughts.

When we arrived at the cave, Wawokiye told Waoka to remain by the entrance while he alone carried me inside. Holding a torch to light the way, he brought me to the deepest chamber of the cave, but I have no memory of when he laid me on a blanket on the floor or when he turned to leave.

I lay with my eyes closed for I know not how long, nor do I know when day passed into night. When first I opened my eyes I was alone in the cave. A sight struck my eyes that I cannot fully describe, so greatly did it fill me with wonder and awe, like watching a star-filled sky on the clearest summer night. A galaxy of stars studded the gloom around me, some so small they were barely visible, some as large as the moon, and in the reflection of the torch's light they glittered like a curtain of jewels.

I saw that the chamber where I lay was large and circular, the floor smooth and nearly level. The sides and ceiling, which stretched about twelve feet above me, were ablaze with nuggets of crystal as transparent as the clearest ice. It was a sight beyond my imagining, so wondrous in its beauty. I never expect to see its like again in my lifetime.

Not far from where I lay on the floor of the cave, a clear stream of water ran through the chamber, disappearing beneath the far wall. Feeling thirsty from the fever, I knelt beside the stream and drank its water which was so pure and cold the fever seemed to disappear almost immediately. Whereupon I stretched out on the blanket and fell fast asleep with only the sound of the running water to break the immense silence.

When next I opened my eyes there appeared before me the form of a man shrouded in darkness against the light from the walls so that I had no vision of his face. In his hands he held a bottle of water taken from the clear stream beside me. He spoke kind and reassuring words, consoling me for my pain and the fever. He bathed the wound in my leg with the water, whispering words I could not understand. Then he faded into the gloom of the central chamber and I slept again.

When I awoke I was amazed to discover my leg no longer throbbed. Upon arising, I found I could put my full weight on it and it never hurt me afterward.

Shortly thereafter Wawokiye appeared to take me from the cave, for two days and two nights had passed without my knowing it. He was not surprised that I was able to walk from the cave easily and lightly.

Often I have thought of the crystal cave, and writing of it fills me with wonder, for I know that in the cave I came face to face with the power of Wakan-Tanka. Strange to say, it was after my journey to the cave that I received the gift of hearing the spirit's voice. But the greatest gift was entering the cave itself. No one, not even a chief, may enter unless it is decreed by *Wicasa-Wakan*.

*

Rachel laid the pen beside the jar of ink and slowly closed the book. She had written the story. Now it would not be lost. But she would never talk about it. To speak of it would be like telling a sacred dream. The magic would disappear in a puff of smoke to be lost in the heavens forever.

She set the pen and ink on the shelf by the door and put the exercise book in the wooden box that Peter had made for her. Pulling the shawl tighter around her, she moved close to the fire. She felt cold, and yet her face burned as well as her throat. Was it possible she had been brought home only to sicken and waste away?

Here there would be no *Wicasa-Wakan*, no crystal cave nor stream to wash away the fever and the pain. The evil *wakan* still lurked in the house, and with its presence no visions would appear, no hidden knowledge of things to come, no healing power.

She must heal herself, then drive the evil *wakan* out. But most of all, she must discover once again the mystery of the crystal cave and the power of Wakan-Tanka. In this house where his spirit was not welcome, she must open the door and invite it to enter.

13

To her great disappointment Rachel missed the breaking out and could only watch from the window as the line of wagons, two abreast and three deep, made its way down the road. A few days later her fever and sore throat abated, and by the end of the week Nina gave her leave to venture outside. Although she resumed her daily journey across town before the second week was over, she felt a certain lassitude, a heaviness in her limbs that made her knees ache. The shadow of an unnamed fear crept along the edges of her thoughts.

In the first week of February Aunt Sarah began to cough, at first just a dry little cough that seemed to come from her throat, but over the next few weeks it deepened. In late winter it settled in her chest.

The doctor prescribed some medicine; for a time the cough diminished but then returned with greater ferocity. The prolonged spasms racked Aunt Sarah's frail body, sapping her little remaining strength. Now when Rachel arrived at the house, more and more often she found her aunt in bed.

On a gray afternoon early in March, Rachel tiptoed

into her aunt's bedroom, careful not to disturb the figure resting in the dark. In a few minutes she would have to give her a spoonful of the brown medicine the doctor had just delivered. Setting the bottle on the chest of drawers opposite the bed, she gazed into the mirror that hung above it.

She had never seen a mirror before coming to Aunt Sarah's house. Her father called them frivolous, a mark of inordinate vanity, and would not permit one in his house. Never before in her life had she seen her own face so clearly, only the image mirrored in Nina's little piece of polished metal or reflected in the streams where ripples of the moving water had distorted her features and where twigs and leafs floating on the surface had blemished her face.

Leaning closer across the dresser top she examined her face in the angle of light that spilled through half-closed shutters. Both Leah and Nina had called her pretty, but as she gazed at the wide gray eyes, the high forehead and prominent cheekbones, she saw only the close resemblance to her father.

She lifted her eyes past her reflected image to the figure on the bed beneath the quilt. How still it was! Like the body of someone who lies in death. She closed her eyes against the sight, but in the darkness a vision of the graveyard beyond the church appeared. Near her mother's stone, another grave opened, a cavernous hole awaiting its burden while beyond a circle of dark-clad people stood in silence. *It is time. Soon now*, a voice whispered to those who waited by the grave.

"No, it mustn't be!" Rachel cried aloud and opened

her eyes to drive away the vision. Surely those whispered words would prove false! But she knew too well that the voice of the spirit spoke only the truth. She lifted one white hand from the quilt and held it gently between her own, pressing the warmth of her own life into the thin fingers. "Don't die, Aunt Sarah, please don't die," she whispered. "I've just found you again."

The figure stirred beneath the covers and Aunt Sarah blinked against the half-shuttered ribbons of light that crisscrossed the stripes of the coverlet.

"I didn't mean to wake you, Aunt Sarah, but the doctor has brought your medicine." She tried to smile reassuringly.

Aunt Sarah rose on one elbow, attempting to sit up, and Rachel tucked another pillow beneath her shoulders. "What I need most is a dose of good fresh air. The house is so close, it's hard to draw a good breath." Aunt Sarah's voice had grown as thin as her body, and the rush of words brought on another spasm of coughing. Rachel poured a spoonful of the brown liquid and held it to her aunt's lips.

"Here, Aunt Sarah. At least it will help soothe your throat."

Her aunt grimaced as she swallowed the medicine. She leaned back against the pillows, lying with hands clasped on her chest, elbows extended like the wings of a chicken.

"I wish I knew what's wrong with me," she said with a deep sigh. "For all that I had to endure with the Comanche, at least I never lost my health. Now I wonder if I shall ever get better."

"You mustn't even think such a thing, Aunt Sarah! Of course you'll get better. It's because this winter has been so cold and damp. The doctor says you'll be better as soon as spring comes."

"Then I must hope that spring comes early this year. Help me up now," she said as she gripped Rachel's arm. "I'd like to be dressed when Nathan gets home. I'm sure the doctor's right. I need only for spring to come."

"You'll see, Aunt Sarah. Before the wild roses bud, you'll be up and dancing again!"

*

In late afternoon Peter unexpectedly appeared at the door.

"I never see you anymore!" he complained to Rachel as he stomped the snow off his boots and stepped into the kitchen.

"You sound just like Leah and Daniel!" Rachel laughed at the petulant look on his face.

"I don't blame them. I've been worried about you. They told me you were sick."

"I feel fine now!" she protested, but his concern warmed her.

"Well, you look pale. You're working too hard. If you won't take care of yourself, I'll just have to do it for you." An unrepressed smile turned up the corners of his mouth. "I plan to start by escorting you home."

"But . . ."

A firm hand on her elbow stilled her protest as he steered her toward the door. "No buts about it. I saw Nathan in town. He was just on his way, so Sarah won't be alone more than a minute." He lifted her cloak from its peg, wrapped it around her. "Put your boots on, girl. It's time to go home!"

"Now you sound like Father," she grumbled but bent to pull on her boots and lace them up. "Aunt Sarah's sleeping. I won't wake her to say good-bye." She pulled on her mittens and stepped out into the cold afternoon.

Halfway down the path she slipped on a patch of ice and would have lost her footing altogether if Peter had not grabbed her arm in time to steady her.

"Whoa! I said you needed looking after, but I didn't think it would mean saving life and limb!" He grinned down at her and continued to hold her arm as they stepped into the road and turned toward town.

"It's these leather boots," she said, looking down at them with distaste. "I'll never get used to them." She yearned for her deerskin boots. They would never slip on the ice.

"Shouldn't you try to get used to things around here, Rachel?" he asked, his gentle voice softening the words. "It would go easier for you if you didn't always look back."

"Oh, now you sound just like everyone else!" Sudden anger flamed but she shook her head with impatience at the too familiar response. "I have tried, Peter," she said in a calmer voice, "but nothing seems to change."

"Perhaps because you don't want it to." With effort she swallowed the sharp retort before her words erupted. He was right of course. They walked on in silence.

"You know, Rachel," he continued, "sometimes I think you try to punish your father just because he brought you home."

"That's not true, Peter!" she protested. "How can you say such a thing?" But even as she spoke the words of denial, her heart told her there was truth in what he said. Perhaps that was why he angered her so often: he told her what she didn't want to hear and he spoke the truth.

"Let's not quarrel, Rachel. I didn't come to fight with you." His words evoked a strange misgiving. He had never before stopped by to walk home with her. Why had he come today? She wanted to ask but was afraid.

As they neared the church Peter veered suddenly. "Let's take the shortcut," he said and directed her across the churchyard into the stand of pines that sheltered the graves beyond. She hadn't walked here since the morning shortly after her arrival when Leah had shown her their mother's grave.

The sight of the carved stones and the knowledge of what was buried in the earth beneath left her with a feeling of desolation. The image of Aunt Sarah rose and nagged her with earlier fears. Midway on the path she stopped and pressed her face against the rough bark of a pine tree, wrapping her arms around its trunk.

"Rachel, what's the matter?" Peter stopped beside her, and his arms went around her as he turned her to face him, clasping her tight until her cheek pressed into the fabric of his coat. It was softer than the bark of the tree but just as sturdy and Rachel cleaved to it.

"What is it?" he asked again, his voice sharp with concern. "I didn't mean to upset you."

Rachel looked up at him, and the anxiety on his face filled her with remorse.

"Oh you haven't, Peter! Not you. It's Aunt Sarah."

"Is she much worse?"

"She's going to die, Peter." Her voice shook with the heavy burden of foreknowledge. "She's going to die quite soon."

"You mustn't think that, Rachel! She'll get better. It'll just take time."

"She's going to die, Peter," Rachel repeated, and this time her voice was steady. "This is something I know. Don't ask me how, I just know. She's not going to get well, and without her I shall be alone."

"You can't think that, Rachel!" He spoke the words softly against her hair, his arms cradling her tenderly.

Rachel thought of White Hawk, of standing close to him as he wrapped his blanket around them in the traditional gesture of courtship. In the months before she had been taken away, he had more often sought her out in the sheltering darkness of nightfall. She had looked forward to those times of privacy. Within the safe circle of his blanket, she could feel his body close to hers even as she now felt Peter's firm body as she leaned against him.

"I'm here." Peter's voice whispered in her ear and White Hawk faded into the darkness of the past. "I'm here and I want to take care of you."

Something in his voice made her breath catch in her throat. She stood motionless, waiting for the bright fragments of time to shift in the winter air and settle into some familiar pattern.

His fingers smoothed the tendrils of hair framing her

face beneath her hood. His lips alighted where his fingers had touched, so soft that for a moment she wondered if she had really felt them. They followed the line of her hair downward to her cheek. Her legs trembled, her blood raced to her heart. Her body urged her forward, wanting to be held, craving the warmth of Peter's body, the protection of his arms.

Slowly his lips brushed across her cheek and sought her lips in return.

Although Rachel's body yearned to be loved, her heart cried out that it could not be. Aunt Sarah's words drummed an insistent beat against the throbbing of her blood. *You must try to understand or it will be hard for you.* The words thrummed along her veins, signaling her to heed the warning. To accept Peter's kiss without telling him, without letting him know what had happened to her would be dishonest, a betrayal of them both.

Ever so slightly, just as she had seen Uncle Nathan do, she turned her face aside and without seeming to do so avoided Peter's kiss. Within the circle of his arms, she drew a deep breath and took a step backward.

Slowly he released her, looking at her quizzically. "Feel better now?" he asked and she nodded, averting her eyes. "You mustn't feel alone, Rachel. That's why I came for you this afternoon." His voice was urgent.

Alarmed, she looked up and met his eyes. "What is it, Peter? Has something happened?"

"No. At least nothing bad. I've been offered the chance to go to Texas, to do surveying there."

Rachel's heart fell within her. Another friend gone.

She had known him such a short time, but she would miss him more than she might have dreamed. His absence would be another death to bear.

She tried to smile, but "That's fine, Peter," was all she could respond. This job would be important to him, a young man just starting out. Instead of regretting her loss she should rejoice at his good fortune, but she could not. "Will you be gone a long time?"

"Yes, a long time. A lot of people will be moving to Texas now that it's become a state. They'll be looking for new land opportunities. Surveyors will be needed there for many years."

"How wonderful for you. You'll do well, I know." She looked away, unable to meet his eyes, fearing he would see the sadness of another loss reflected in hers. "Will you be leaving soon?"

"Not for a while yet. Another eight or ten weeks if I go. I don't have to decide right away, but I wanted to tell you. I thought it might make a difference—there would be time for you to think about it." He took her hand and pulled her to him again, searching her eyes. "I would like not to go alone, Rachel," he said softly.

It was more than she could bear. The sense of loss deepened within her. It would be so easy to say yes, to tell him she would go with him to Texas where no one would know her story. It's not easy for any of us, Aunt Sarah had told her. No, not for any of them, not Uncle Nathan, not her father. And Peter? How hard would it be for him, and how would she find the courage to tell him what he had to know? She could not deceive him. Somehow she must find the courage to speak.

But his touch locked the words within her, and gently she withdrew her hand from his. Turning away, she gazed past the churchyard, beyond the road, searching for the words among the clouds above the horizon. "There are things I must tell you," she said at last.

The enormity of what she must say left her feeling cold and empty.

"Don't say anything right now, Rachel. I know I've taken you by surprise. We've been friends, but I have . . . have grown so fond of you. I want you to think about me as more than a friend if you can."

Tears sprang to her eyes at his gentle plea and she drew a deep breath against the knot in her chest. "You've been so good to me, Peter, it would be easy to think of you as more than a friend. But to become a wife, if that's what you're wanting, is not as easy. Before you say more, hear me and then decide." She fell silent. How could she tell him those things she could not bear to say even to herself?

She turned to face him, lifting her chin, holding her back erect. She would not feel shame before him no matter how hard it was to speak the truth.

"I have been taken by an Indian brave," she said and lifted her head higher. "Not once but many times." She looked him full in the face and spoke in a rush before he could respond. "On the journey north, after I was taken from the fort, the brave who captured me . . . he lay with me, Peter."

The words seared her throat, burned her face. But she would not lose courage now. "Can you think how it would be, Peter, to love a woman who has been taken by an Indian brave, how it would feel to hold your arms around my body that has been—"

She stopped to search his eyes and saw a myriad of unspoken feelings pass across his face like the shadows of the wind-tossed clouds across the landscape. He stood motionless and silent.

Relentlessly she drove herself onward. "Think carefully, Peter. Would you want a wife who has been intimate with an Indian in every way?"

In the open book of his face she read his response, the horror, the pity, and, she could not pretend otherwise, the revulsion. It was fleeting perhaps, but there all the same, the shadow in the eyes, the almost imperceptible drawing away.

Without speaking he had answered her, had snatched out her heart and trampled it. Her legs felt too weak to support her. She wanted to cry out that she was still Rachel, could still be loved as a woman, but the flame she had felt as he held her in his arms was already flickering out. It would not be rekindled. She was drained of feeling, but she would stand tall before him and meet his eyes without shame, without seeking pity.

"It's all right, Rachel. It doesn't matter," he said in a voice so quiet she had to bend her head to hear him. "That was long ago. It doesn't change how I feel about you."

"Perhaps not now, but someday it would, Peter, I know it." She echoed Aunt Sarah's words. "You would grow to hate me."

"I couldn't hate you, Rachel!" he protested. "I want

to protect you from all that." But he remained where he was, an arm's length from where she stood.

"But that's not possible anymore!" An unexpected thought startled her. "You know, it's strange, but when Father looks at me he sees an obedient daughter who bends to his will. When you look at me, Peter, you see someone who needs your protection. But I am neither of those persons. I'm not a timid rabbit. I'm not sweet and good like Leah. I'm not the one for you."

Surprised at her own sudden discovery, Rachel almost smiled. "There, you see, it is really Leah whom you should love. She's exactly as you want her to be. Besides, Peter, you're too kind to be burdened with someone who would make you miserable." Reaching out one mittened hand, she gently touched his cheek. She looked at him through misted lashes and forced a smile. "Even if you didn't grow to hate me, we would not be right for each other."

"Perhaps," was all he said. "Perhaps," he repeated after a moment's thought, but he reached for her hand and held it lightly in his.

Together they turned down the path, walking hand in hand. The churchyard lay quiet behind them as they stepped out into the road. The arc of the sun dipped beneath the horizon. The wind dropped to a quiet whisper. Even the pine trees barely stirred.

"Why did you tell me, Rachel?" he asked after they had walked a few minutes without speaking. "I might never have known if you hadn't told me."

"But I would have known, Peter, and the knowledge

would have lived with me every day we were together. It would have eaten at our table and lain between us in bed. Before long it would have poisoned the very air in our house."

Without speaking he drew her arm through his. As the afternoon moved into evening, they walked along the road in silence. For a few minutes she had wanted to believe Peter might be the one for her, the one she could love without shame or fear of restraints upon the heart. How easily she could have deceived herself! She had closed her eyes to the truth because she had not looked deeply enough into her own heart. It should not surprise her then that others could not perceive what lay hidden there.

Peter spoke no more about what she had revealed and she was thankful, relieved he hadn't expressed anger or offered pity. Perhaps his silence came only from an inability to find adequate words, but even so she was grateful. Anger or pity would only renew the shame.

She had spoken the truth. It had opened the trap around her heart and released the pain. She thought of the morning she had stood with Leah by their mother's grave fearing the presence of the evil *wakan*. Now, for the first time since she had come to this town, the spirits no longer threatened. She had laid those demons to rest. Her heart felt almost at ease.

14

"You see, the doctor was right!" Aunt Sarah stood alone in the center of the kitchen and smiled at Rachel in the doorway, while across the room Uncle Nathan mirrored the smile.

Speechless, Rachel stood in the open doorway, her eyes fixed on her aunt in amazement until she remembered to close the door against the chilly breeze behind her.

It hardly seemed possible that such a transformation could take place in such a short time. She had not been at their house for four days. It was the week before Palm Sunday, and Nina had needed her at home for the spring cleaning before the coming of Easter.

"Her cough's gone!" Uncle Nathan said, his voice conveying his happiness. "We had our first warm days this week, and look!"—he snapped his fingers in the air as if to emphasize the miracle—"the cough has disappeared!"

"Just as the doctor said it would!" Aunt Sarah repeated, still smiling at the wonder of it.

"I'm so glad, Aunt Sarah!" Rachel exclaimed. "It's hard to believe!"

Even as she spoke, unwelcome doubt crept in, settling

in the pit of her stomach. No matter how she might wish it, no doctor had the power to say what would come to be. The voice of the spirit had told her otherwise.

Aunt Sarah sat on the settle. "But you mustn't think I don't still need you," she said somewhat breathlessly. Although her smile had faded only slightly, perspiration beaded her forehead. "I still tire easily, and I know it will be a while before I get my full strength back. The doctor says I mustn't overdo, so I do hope you'll still come." Her eyes pleaded with Rachel.

"Of course I will!"

If only she could believe it truly was a miraculous recovery! But doubt still plagued her. Aunt Sarah looked pale and dark circles ringed her eyes. But now that the cough had disappeared, perhaps in time Aunt Sarah would heal completely. Perhaps it was only her own concern for her aunt that had spoken those fearful words.

She should rejoice and hope that with the coming of spring the healing would quicken, just as the trees which had so long appeared dead were now beginning to hint at the new life rising within them.

*

"In the name of the Father, Son and Holy Ghost." Head bowed, the Reverend Mr. Porter paused before addressing his congregation, then raised his head and the gathering of people grew still.

"On this Palm Sunday, as we approach the holy day when Jesus rose again to sit on the right hand of God the Father, it behooves us to remember the nature and importance of the Trinity."

He cast a warning eye upon the congregation. Beginning at the farthest corner of the small church, it swept forward across the lifted faces to the first pew where it fixed upon Rachel. He bent once more to the sheets of handwritten text before him.

The night before he had predicted the size of today's congregation. "We'll need extra chairs tomorrow," he had said with a sigh. "On the Sunday before Easter, they'll all be in church. It's the last-minute pilgrimage of backsliders hoping to assure their place in heaven."

His prediction had proved right. The church was crowded. Even extra chairs set in the aisle could not accommodate the overflow gathering. And now he had their full attention. Not even a cough or a rustle distracted from his message.

"Too often," he continued, the twin red-gold arches of his eyebrows rising with the level of his voice, "too often we celebrate the death and rebirth of our Lord Jesus without pausing to consider the third part of the Trinity. For the meaning of God extends beyond mere belief in the Father and the Son. We must never forget the significance of that most important third part of the Trinity, for it is in the understanding of the nature of the Holy Ghost that the full power and mystery of the Trinity rests. The Two are not complete without acceptance of the Third."

The sun shone full in the window, casting a narrow path of light across the front of the pulpit.

"Not to believe in all three as holy is to say that the sun and moon exist but not the stars."

He has forgotten one thing, Rachel thought. He has

forgotten the sky which is the fourth part of sun, moon, and stars. Four is the most magic number of all living things. There are four parts of all being: earth, air, fire, water. Wakan-Tanka has four titles, being called *Great Mystery, Chief God, Creator* and *Decision-Maker*.

There are four parts of time: day, night, month, year. There are four seasons: spring, summer, fall, winter; four times in a man's life: baby, child, adult, old man; four kinds of creatures: flying, crawling, two-legged, four-legged; and four parts of the plant: root, stem, leaves, fruit. And all flow together, moving one into the other in the great circle of life.

In his sermons her father often spoke of the Devil or Satan. Perhaps he had left him out of the Trinity. Could it be that Satan was the fourth part? She would have to ask him sometime.

Beside her, Leah sat in her usual place, and beyond Leah's lap Rachel could see the outline of Peter's long legs under the dark serge of his Sunday trousers. He sat beside Leah every Sunday now and came even more often to visit. If Rachel happened not to be at home when he came, she later heard every detail from Leah: Peter had held the skein of wool for her to wind, so patient, his strong hands so gentle; he played a song he had composed just for her on his harmonica; he laughed with her about some silly thing and remarked on how much alike they thought; he had placed his hand on the back of her neck, and she had felt so weak she thought she might faint.

When Peter had first turned his attention to Leah, little seeds of envy took root in Rachel's thoughts. But when she saw how much Leah loved him and how impossible it was for her to mask her love, she couldn't begrudge Leah Peter's full attention. She could never mar her sister's happiness. Nothing would be worth bearing that burden, and when she saw Leah and Peter together, she was more than ever convinced she had spoken the truth: no one could make Peter a better wife than Leah.

Rachel had said nothing about Peter's move to Texas. That news was for him to make known when he was ready. She was sure it was only a question of time before he asked Leah to marry him. Perhaps he was waiting until his plans were more certain.

*

On the Monday before Easter, the winds shifted from the northwest to south, and the warm air blew from Texas into Missouri, drying the land, melting the few remaining pockets of snow.

In the yard behind the house, Rachel stooped to gather another armful of dirty linen and dropped it into the washtub steaming over the fire. Beside her, Leah grasped the long wooden paddle with both hands and pulled it through the tub, moving the bedclothes back and forth through the hot, soapy water.

Every now and then the stirring stopped and Leah gazed out across the yard into the distance. Rachel smiled to herself. At the rate they were going, she doubted they would finish by sundown. But it would do no good to try to hurry Leah. Clearly her sister's mind was not on the wash!

She touched Leah lightly on the arm. "Look," she said

and pointed to a robin building its nest in the apple tree only a few yards away.

"What? Oh, yes," Leah responded vaguely and bent over the tub to renew her stirring.

"No, no, Leah!" Rachel laughed aloud at her sister's distraction. "Not the wash. The robin. Over there in the apple tree. Look, he's building his nest with a strand of wool from your shawl."

At daybreak the air had been raw and chilly, but by the time the sun was fully risen they had shed their wraps. Now they stood bare armed, the warmth of the sun and the heat of the fire making their faces rosy and damp with perspiration.

"A penny for your thoughts, Leah," Rachel teased. "Or aren't they fit to hear?" She laughed at the blush that deepened the color in Leah's cheeks. Her sister had never looked so pretty. How good it was to see her so happy, so alive!

"Not fit indeed! For shame, Rachel!" Leah lifted the wet paddle over Rachel and shook a shower of drops onto her head. "I'll make a Christian of you yet! I baptize thee Miss Holier-Than-Thou!"

Laughing, Rachel snatched a wet pillowcase from the wooden trough that held the finished wash and flung it at her sister. Leah squealed as the sodden cloth landed on her head.

"You'll be sorry!" Waving the paddle wildly in the air, she chased Rachel around the fire.

"Leah, don't you dare!" Rachel shrieked while the forgotten pillowcase was trampled into the dirt.

At that moment Peter appeared around the corner of

the yard. Both girls stopped short, Rachel with one foot on the muddy pillowcase, Leah with the paddle still raised above her head.

"Nina said you were out working," Peter said, grinning at their embarrassment. "If this is work, I hate to think what would happen if you two decided to play!"

"Ha!" Rachel retorted. "Some people who sit around all day with nothing to do don't know what real work is!" She picked up the muddy pillowcase and hastily deposited it back into the boiling water.

Leah stood where she was with the paddle, too confused for any retort. Peter lifted it from her hands. "Here," he said, handing it to Rachel. "Do penance with this for your sins. I want to talk to Leah." Taking Leah by the arm, he led her across the yard to the small shed where their father stabled their horse.

Rachel's eyes followed them. Peter's face grew serious and he held Leah's hand as he talked to her. Leah gazed up at him, silent, wide-eyed.

Rachel turned away. It hurt to watch them, so engrossed was each in the other. There was only one reason for Peter to come in the middle of the day. He had made his decision.

Desire filled the emptiness Rachel felt, a longing for someone to look at her with that same intensity, to hold her close, shutting out the rest of the world. But no white man would ever look at her like that. She thought of White Hawk and the longing deepened.

She looked past the shed into the open fields that stretched for more than two miles between their house and the narrow stand of cottonwoods that lined the

Missouri River. By now the tribe would be coming down from the mountains to the open prairie. It was time for the burning-off, the event that marked an end of winter and the coming of spring, the renewal of all life.

In a great, snaking line the braves from many tribes would join to wind across the plains, burning the old grass before them, preparing the earth for the new grass to come. How clearly she remembered the first time she had witnessed the burning of the dried grass in a great wave of fire that left only a blackened stubble in its wake. She had not believed that anything could grow from such desolation; but before the sun had set seven times, new grass appeared, covering the scorched earth with tiny pale-green shoots that transformed the land into a blanket of green. The wonder of seeing the prairie restored each spring had never left her.

She lifted her head and inhaled deeply to catch a distant scent of burning grass, but only the odor of lye soap and steaming clothes rose to greet her.

One by one she lifted the sheets out of the tub and dropped them in the trough to cool. She and Leah would twist the ends of the cloth to wring out the water and hang them on the line to dry. Such a strange way to mark the greening of the land, this washing of the winter bedclothes.

Out of the corner of her eye she looked toward Leah and Peter. He took Leah in his arms and bent his head to kiss her. Leah's face did not turn aside but lifted to meet his lips fully with her own.

As Peter released her, he spoke and Leah smiled and nodded. When he turned to go, his eye met Rachel's and held it. With a smile and quick wave of the hand, he was gone.

In a trance Leah turned toward Rachel.

Rachel had no need to ask what had passed between them. Leah's face told her all. Peter would be going to Texas soon now. He had asked Leah to go with him, to set out to this new country as his wife. And Leah had accepted. All they needed was her father's blessing which he would gladly give, for he looked on Peter as a son.

Leah and Peter would go to Texas. Only little Daniel and Aunt Sarah would remain—and herself. A year from now, which of the three would still be here? Rachel shivered under the warm spring sun.

"Oh, Rachel!" Leah called. "Rachel, you'll never guess what's happened. Wait until I tell you!"

As Rachel watched Leah run toward her, her chin lifted and held steady. Her arms reached out, ready to welcome her sister's embrace.

15

Through half-closed eyes Rachel peered up at the bowed heads gathered around the table. Platters of roasted venison, red potatoes, spring greens boiled with ham hocks, and buttermilk biscuits waited for her father's blessing. Across the table Daniel's nose twitched at the rich aroma of gravy in front of him.

"On this Easter day," the Reverend Porter intoned, "we ask Your special blessing and give thanks to Thee for all Thy bounties."

April, the Moon of the Birth of Calves. Everywhere across the northern prairie the buffalo cows would be birthing until the plains were filled with nursing calves.

Daniel's chin started to creep upward but as their father's voice continued, he settled it against his chest. "We thank Thee for gathering our family together to commemorate the resurrection of our Blessed Savior."

Only Jamie was missing; even Aunt Sarah was here, the first time she had eaten with them since Christmas. Rachel could hear Aunt Sarah coughing again, and every few minutes her aunt raised her handkerchief to her lips. It troubled Rachel, although no one else seemed to notice the quiet, dry exhalation of air from the back of her throat, more of a continual clearing than a cough.

Although the doctor still predicted a complete recovery, Aunt Sarah seemed to make little progress in regaining her strength. When pressed to name her strange ailment, the doctor had only shaken his head and called it a general malaise—what else it might be, he really couldn't say. But as the light of the afternoon sun fell across the table, the spiderweb of lines that etched Aunt Sarah's pale skin seemed both darker and deeper.

"We ask thee, O Lord, to bless the coming marriage of my daughter Leah and Peter Ellsworth. May their life together be long and fruitful."

Peter turned his head to glance at Leah beside him. She had not stopped smiling since her father had given his consent. Now she responded to Peter's look by pressing her shoulder against his. If only White Hawk could sit beside her now with his shoulder against hers! Sudden longing caught Rachel's breath, and she looked away.

Pausing to clear his thoat, her father turned his eyes upon her. Hastily she bent her head.

"On this day of resurrection, O Lord, we thank Thee for the return of our daughter, Rachel, and for granting her new life."

Daniel looked up at her and smiled. His lips formed the word "Amen" and she almost laughed aloud. At least she could still enjoy his young arms around her when he hugged her.

Her father closed his eyes; the blessing was drawing to a close.

"We thank Thee, Lord, for Thy bountiful gifts. In the name of the Father, Son and Holy Ghost. Amen."

"Amen," a chorus of voices responded and dishes of food passed from hand to hand. The naming of the Trinity reminded Rachel of her question.

"Father," she said after the platters of food had made their way around the table, "something puzzles me."

His mouth full of venison, her father looked up, his eyebrows lifting quizzically as he waited for her question.

"Could it be, Father," she continued, "that Satan is the fourth part of the Trinity, for it must be incomplete with only three?"

His mouth stopped chewing, his lips parted slightly as he stared at her. Then, with deliberation, he continued chewing.

Around the table there was silence. Leah fixed her eyes on her plate. Daniel and Aunt Sarah stared at Rachel, eyes wide with apprehension. Beside Rachel, Uncle Nathan coughed and reached for his glass of water. Only Peter looked amused, a slight quirk of his lips forming a smile he tried to swallow. Raising his napkin to his mouth, he dabbed at a nonexistent smear of grease.

Nina was the first to break the silence.

"There is no fourth being in the Trinity, Rachel," she said in a quiet voice. "Only the forces of good are part of the Godhead. Perhaps you weren't aware that Satan is the power of evil?"

"Oh, yes, I know that," Rachel replied. She looked at her father and saw anger blaze in his eyes. Why would her words make him angry? She was only asking about something she didn't understand.

"Four is the most magic number of all living things," she said, trying to explain her question. "Whatever is powerful in the universe is only one part of four. As the sky is the fourth part of sun, moon, and stars." She repeated the example of the trinity her father had used in his sermon a week ago.

He swallowed the meat and slowly lowered his fork to his plate. He spoke without raising his voice, but although his voice was quiet, his lips tightened, his nostrils flared. "That may well be a heathen belief, but it is no part of the Christian faith."

Rachel met her father's eyes but did not respond. Let him say what he would, this time she would not be the one who provoked dissension!

"Do you know what blasphemy is, Rachel?" he asked. Without waiting for her reply he turned to his son. His voice was as hard and biting as the sharp edge of the flesher she kept hidden under a pile of clothes. "Tell your sister, Daniel! Tell Rachel what it is to blaspheme against the teachings of the church!"

Daniel shrank in his chair and looked at Rachel. She tried to smile at him in a reassuring way.

"Yes, please tell me, Daniel," she said. She knew very well the meaning of blasphemy: one could not sit week after week beneath the onslaught of her father's sermons and not know what it was to blaspheme. But this time she would not let Daniel become the quarry caught in the snare between them.

Without taking his eyes from hers, he responded in a small voice. "to speak with ir . . . irreverence." He stumbled over the word but continued without a pause, repeating the phrases he had faithfully memorized. "To act in a profane manner against the beliefs of the holy church."

"Ah, yes," she said still smiling at him. "Now I understand. Thank you, Daniel." She stiffened, waiting for her father's response.

"Better you should thank God for saving you from the perdition of those heathen beliefs!" His voice lashed out at her.

"Enough, Tobias!" The sharpness of Nina's rebuke startled Rachel, but her stepmother continued in a gentler voice. "Rachel's question was an honest one, I believe, Tobias. How else can she relearn her Christian lessons?"

Rachel sat rigid, waiting for her father to lash out again. He looked around the table and the tight line of his lips relaxed. "You're right, my dear," he said, "and we'll all profit by your reminder." He turned his attention once more to his plate. Beside her, Rachel felt Uncle Nathan draw a sigh of relief. The storm had been averted, and they could enjoy their dinner in peace. She was thankful the day would not be spoiled.

But her relief was short lived.

Without warning Aunt Sarah coughed again, not the quick, dry scraping of air in the throat, but a prolonged, rattling cough to clear thick mucus from deep in the chest. Rachel's stomach churned in fear and she hunched her shoulders against her ears to shut out the dreaded sound. Dear God, not now, not yet!

A chair crashed to the floor. The sharp crack of splintering wood punctuated Uncle Nathan's cry.

"Sarah! My God, what's wrong?"

Rachel forced her eyes to focus on Aunt Sarah's place. The food on her plate was untouched. Aunt Sarah stood above it, hands grasping the edge of the table, fingers so taut the knuckles stood out white and bony against the dark polished wood.

"Sarah, what is it!" Nina jumped up from the table. At the fear in her stepmother's voice, Rachel raised her eyes to her aunt's face; but where her features should have been Rachel saw instead the fixed, dark eye of the open grave.

The staring eye slowly closed. In its place her aunt's face gradually reappeared. Her mouth was open but no words came, only a rasping intake of air deep in her throat as she tried to draw a breath through the thick fluid in her lungs. Her face was bluish-white, almost translucent, like the thin skin of ice over water in winter. The pale face wavered behind her hand clasping her taut white throat.

"Aunt Sarah, what's wrong?" Rachel heard another voice cry, perhaps her own, and the cry released her. In one swift motion she left her chair and moved toward her aunt just as Aunt Sarah started to fall. Uncle Nathan was there before her, grasping his wife, lifting her in his arms before her knees could touch the ground.

"Put her on our bed, Nathan," Nina's voice directed. Gently, he carried her into the next room and laid her on the eiderdown quilt that covered the bed. Still clasping her throat, Aunt Sarah struggled to draw a breath. Nina propped two pillows behind her.

"Rachel, help support her," Nina ordered. "Leah, fetch a cold cloth."

Rachel sat on the side of the bed, reaching one arm behind her aunt's neck to keep her head erect. Nina sat across from her, unfastening the buttons on Aunt Sarah's blouse, the new one Uncle Nathan had given her for Easter, embroidered with violets. Uncle Nathan knelt beside the bed, holding one of her white hands between his two rough, reddened ones.

Rachel felt the frail shoulders shake. "She's shivering, Nina," she said, helpless, and looked up to see Leah returning from the kitchen with a wet cloth.

Before Leah could give Nina the cloth, Sarah's body suddenly convulsed. In one terrible racking cough a gush of mucus and blood erupted from her throat, spreading a great red stain across the front of her blouse and onto the quilt. She arched her neck, turning her head away from Rachel.

"My God, Sarah, what's happening?" Uncle Nathan's cry reverberated in the small room.

Before Nina could wipe the bloodied face with the wet cloth, a second cough followed and another gush of blood stained the white pillow.

Aunt Sarah's face was gray.

"Nina! What can we do?" Uncle Nathan shouted, but Rachel knew his question was futile. She sat frozen, paralyzed by the certainty that nothing could be done. She had heard the spirit's voice and it had spoken true. How foolish to have hoped otherwise! It only made Aunt Sarah's dying harder to bear!

Tears streamed down her face as she cradled Aunt

Sarah's head in her arms and pressed her wet cheek against her aunt's disheveled hair. Aunt Sarah's lips parted and Rachel closed her eyes, fearing another gush of the thick, dark fluid, but this time Aunt Sarah spoke. Her eyes were glazed, unfocused; the voice was hesitant but clear.

"Oh-my-dear-I-am-so-sorry." She breathed a great sigh, and fell back against Rachel's arm. Her eyes closed.

"No!" Uncle Nathan cried and pulled his wife's blood-stained body into his arms. "I'm the one! Forgive *me,* Sarah! It's I—I who am so very sorry!"

Her uncle's cry unknotted the grief and pain within Rachel. She fell to her knees beside the bed, burying her face in the folds of the quilt.

In the darkness a hand touched the top of her head, and her father's voice spoke softly.

"Blessed be he who believeth in the Lord, for He is the Resurrection and Life Everlasting."

Rachel knelt by the bed, her own arms cradling her breast, and she wept for the life that had ended too soon, for the undeserved years of unhappiness her aunt had endured, and for the empty, hollow chambers of her own heart that might never again be filled.

16

Leah and Peter were married on a warm Saturday morning late in May. Only the family was in attendance. The ceremony was simple and quiet, for the marriage followed the funeral of Aunt Sarah more closely than any of them would have liked. But Peter had been called to Texas sooner than expected and Leah would not be left behind.

Adorned in their mother's wedding dress and wearing a veil that crowned her dark hair, Leah stood before her father at the altar of his church, Peter at her side. Rachel held her sister's bouquet of fresh apple blossoms cut from the tree behind the church. With her face glowing, her eyes shining, Leah looked more beautiful than Rachel had ever seen her, and Peter's eyes seldom strayed from his new bride's face.

Rachel pictured herself in Leah's place, standing beside Peter, wearing her mother's veil to tame the red-gold hair that was curling wildly in the warm, humid air. She could have been Peter's bride. As often as she reminded herself that she had been honest in telling him of her ordeal and truthful in stating they were not right for each other, it was hard to watch Leah take her place and cling to his hand as though she wished never to let it go. Rachel tried to put aside the occasional pangs of envy that stirred inside.

The couple knelt as her father prayed above them, and for a moment she tried to imagine how it would be to sleep with a man—or to lie with White Hawk as his wife. The thought took her breath away and she forced her attention to the words of the service. She would not allow herself to dwell on such images just as she willed herself not to think of Aunt Sarah's newly marked grave with the dirt still raw around it. Uncle Nathan's sad face was already a vivid reminder of Aunt Sarah's absence.

"I now pronounce you man and wife." Her father's closing words broke Rachel's reverie. Peter pulled Leah to him and kissed her quickly as the small wedding party gathered around the couple with their congratulations.

After the dimness of the church, Rachel had to squint in the bright morning light and almost dropped the bouquet that Leah threw her from the church steps.

"You'll be next, Rachel!" Leah called, laughing with delight.

"No! Not Rachel! She has to wait for me!" Daniel retorted vehemently and everyone laughed. But when Rachel momentarily caught Peter's eye, he looked away, and she knew he was remembering the shadow that clung to her here in the white man's world.

She braced herself for the departure. Traveling to Texas was an adventure the two would share, the beginning of a new life together in a new state. For Rachel, though, their journey to Texas meant the loss of a sister and her two dearest friends. She turned away from the laughing faces.

The small wedding party returned to the house for a quick wedding breakfast of wheat cakes and sausage which only Daniel ate with relish, helping himself to whatever was left on the platters. Soon it would be time for the couple to set out, for Peter was anxious to begin their long journey.

For the last time Leah and Rachel stood together in the small attic room they shared under the eaves while Leah changed into her traveling clothes. Carefully she folded their mother's wedding dress and packed it in the box where it had been stored with tissue and sprigs of lavender to keep it fresh.

"I'm leaving this for you, Rachel," Leah said, embracing her sister. "I hope you'll wear it someday soon. That would be a wonderful gift, a reason for Peter and me to come home for a visit!"

Rachel held her sister tight and blinked away the tears. She wouldn't spoil Leah's pleasure by telling her how unlikely such an event would be. "You must come home to visit—often," she whispered, "even without a wedding."

"Oh, we will! You can be certain. And just as soon as we're settled, you must come to Texas and stay a long time!" Leah gazed around the attic room. "I remember the first night you came." She smiled at Rachel. "You slept on the floor."

"I thought you didn't know!"

"I woke up early and saw you there, but I didn't want

to say anything. You seemed so—so frightened and timid then. I worried about you."

Rachel laughed at Leah's perception of her. "Frightened perhaps—but hardly timid!"

"But you were so strong. I never told you how I admired the way you stood up to Father. How I envied you! I wished I had your courage."

Rachel hugged her sister to her and caught the faint odor of lavender. "And all the time I was wishing I could learn to be more patient like you!"

"There's something else I must confess," Leah's small voice said in her ear.

"What's that?" Rachel smiled at the notion of Leah confessing some imagined slight.

"I was—well, I was jealous of you and Peter. I tried not to be, but I—I thought you were the one he cared for most."

"Don't be foolish," Rachel said and laughed lightly. "Peter only thinks of me as a sister. You're the one he wanted to marry . . . and I know he loves you very much." She felt the soft skin of Leah's cheek brush against hers and wanted to hold it there.

"There's so much I'm sorry now I didn't say, didn't ask you about," Leah said. "I thought there would be time. And I was afraid."

"Afraid? Of what?"

"Of perhaps hurting you," Leah said, adding, "and also of Father."

"There will be another time to talk. We must promise each other."

Footsteps sounded on the narrow wooden steps. "Leah," Nina's voice called out. "It's time. Peter wants to get started."

"I'm coming right now!" Tears misted Leah's lashes as she held her sister close. "I'm so happy, Rachel!" she whispered, "Thank you for not loving him." For a moment Rachel held her sister hard, not wanting to let her go. Then with lingering regret she released her.

Leah turned and ran down the steps.

The family stood together in the bright spring day and watched the wagon drive from the yard. Daniel ran after it, throwing a handful of rice at Peter and Leah who turned and waved.

"Good-bye, good-bye!" Daniel called, his high child's voice ringing in the clear air.

Rachel stood on the back stoop beside Uncle Nathan. Across the yard her father stood beside Nina, his arm around her waist. Nina leaned lightly into his side. Only Daniel was excited, laughing and calling as he tried to keep up with the trotting horses.

When the wagon pulled into the road, the boy turned and ran back, coming to stand beside Rachel.

"Look what Peter gave me!" From his pocket he pulled a large slingshot fashioned from a smooth piece of wood. "He made it just for me! He said it was a going-away present." His voice rang with pride, a wide smile crinkled his nose.

"How nice of him!" Rachel looked down into his dark eyes. "Now you can go hunting."

"I'll bring you a deer, Rachel," he said. Little lines of worry puckered his forehead. "But not for a going-away present. You won't get married and move away, will you, Rachel? I don't want you to ever go away." He slipped his hand into hers. She held it tightly, unable to answer. She shaded her moist eyes with her hand as she gazed out to the horizon.

Far down the road a little cloud of dust floating in the bright morning air marked Leah and Peter's departure, the only reminder of the wagon now lost from sight. Rachel watched the dust slowly settle and wondered how many more losses she would have to endure.

17

Rachel closed the blue exercise book, the last of the supply Peter had given her.

She had used the final pages to tell about the Sun Dance, a fitting way to come to an end. There would be no more books, but they had served the purpose and what she had written would not be forgotten.

She continued sitting at the table, too weary to face the tasks that awaited her. As hard as she had tried to make the best of things here in St. Joseph, the death of Aunt Sarah and the departure of Peter and Leah had made living in the white man's world even more difficult and lonely.

With each new dawn it was growing harder to leave the warmth of her bed. Before the coming of summer, the cold had never seemed to leave her bones; and even now that the days were hot and sultry, fatigue continued to weigh on her like a heavy load. The knowledge that in the last months of her life, Aunt Sarah had also felt tired all the time weighed on her as well. She tried to push the thought away.

The house was silent: Nina had gone to visit a sick friend, her father was working at church, and Daniel was hunting with his new slingshot. It felt strange to be completely alone, so seldom did it happen.

It was the beginning of the Moon of Ripe Berries, the first of June. The weather was unseasonably warm. Rachel picked up the paper booklet and fanned herself, enjoying the breeze stirred by the fluttering pages. She unfastened the buttons of her shirtwaist and fanned again until the air cooled the damp skin between her breasts where perspiration had gathered. She lifted a hand and cupped her fingers lightly around one breast where it curved upward under the thin cotton chemise, feeling its fullness and the nipple that hardened against her fingertips. Closing her eyes, she gave herself up to the memory of White Hawk, of standing close to him on the night before he left on the last hunt of autumn, the night before she was taken by the white men and put aboard the *Yellowstone*.

White Hawk had talked with her a long time that night, excited about the hunt, promising to bring her the hide of a doe for a new dress and moccasins. He stood very close as they whispered together outside the tipi, not wanting to part, protected by the folds of his blanket from both the eyes of the elders and the chilly night air. His hands held the edges of the blanket, pulling it tighter, drawing her closer until they stood face to face, and his hands, chest high, brushed against her breasts. The light touch of his knuckles as they grazed the curving flesh made her nipples spring to life beneath the soft deerskin that separated his flesh from hers. Or had she imagined that touch, willing it to happen until her thoughts made it so, knowing that when a girl allows a brave to touch her breasts, it's a sign she belongs to him. Had White Hawk's touch been real or only an imagined yearning?

Hurried footsteps sounded on the path, probably Daniel returning from his own small hunt. With a start, Rachel hastily buttoned her dress, managing to fasten all but the top button before Daniel burst into the room.

Breathless with excitement and the exertion of running home, he held up a heavily laden burlap sack, dangling it before her. "Rachel, you'll never guess what I got!"

"Goodness, Daniel, what is it? You look like you're about to burst!"

Daniel plopped the heavy sack on the floor by her feet. "I got a rabbit! With my slingshot! I hit a rabbit with a stone and killed it all by myself!" His face beamed.

"That's wonderful, Daniel!" Her voice echoed his excitement. "Wait till Peter hears. He'll be so pleased. You must write and tell him!"

"Look how big it is!" He opened the top of the sack and dumped the rabbit unceremoniously onto the floor.

"That's just about the biggest rabbit I've ever seen! We'll surprise Nina and fix a great rabbit stew for dinner."

"And you'll show me how to skin it—and how to tan the skin with your—your—that thing I found in the fire?"

"My flesher."

"Yes, your flesher. And then you can show me how to make moccasins!" He was bobbing up and down with anticipation. "Let's do it right now!"

"I'll show you how to skin it, but Father wouldn't like it if you used my flesher. You know he won't let you wear moccasins."

"I don't care. I just want to learn how." He stroked the soft fur of the rabbit. "You promised, Rachel," he said, looking up at her through dark lashes. "You promised to show me how. The very first day you came." Reproachful eyes pleaded with her.

"You're right, Daniel, I did. I had almost forgotten, it seems so long ago." Yet only eight moons had waxed and waned since that first morning. With a sigh she lifted the rabbit to examine it more closely. "Look," she said, pointing to a large red welt behind its left ear. "Here's where your stone hit. It was a good clean shot, one any brave would be proud of." Daniel blushed at her praise, standing on tiptoe to see the wound more clearly.

"Run upstairs and get the flesher while I sharpen the knife," Rachel said. "It's in the chest beneath my wool cloak."

Before she had finished honing the blade on the stone, Daniel reappeared with the flesher in hand.

"Let's go outside," Rachel said, lifting the rabbit by the ears. "Nina wouldn't like us making a mess in her kitchen."

Out in the yard Rachel knelt on a patch of grass.

"Now," she instructed as Daniel stood beside her, leaning over her shoulder for a better view, "all the tools must be just so. The knife must be very sharp or too much flesh will be left on the skin. That's wasteful and means more work!" She tested the blade against the skin of her thumb.

Slowly Rachel began to skin the rabbit, explaining each step to Daniel, demonstrating as she explained. She slit the rabbit the full length of its body and laid it open, carefully removing the brain and all the innards which she placed on a plank lying in the yard. Daniel swallowed hard but kept his eyes on her hands, watching her intently as she separated the skin from the rabbit's flesh.

"We need a wooden bowl," she said looking up from her task, "and a hammer and some small nails." Daniel ran to fetch them while she carried the skinned meat into the cool root cellar. Daniel returned with the necessary items just as she emerged.

Rachel put the rabbit's brain and liver in the bowl and set them aside. Carefully she laid out the skin, flesh side up, stretching it until it was taut. She fastened it in place with the nails, hammering them into the sun-baked earth.

"This is how to hold the flesher," she said, showing him how she gripped the horn handle against her palm so it wouldn't slip. "For a good flesher you need a hard stone with an edge like a razor."

Working on the underside of the skin, she began to scrape it clean, removing what remained of the meat and fat with her flesher. With swift, smooth strokes she scraped the sharp blade of the stone's edge against the hide.

"A good flesher's very valuable," she said as she worked. "An Indian caught stealing someone's flesher is banished from the tribe."

Daniel's eyes grew round. "Even a woman?"

"Oh yes, even a woman."

"Let me try, Rachel," Daniel begged, kneeling beside her.

"Hold it just like a knife," she said, handing him the flesher, "with the sharp edge against the skin." She watched as he pulled it down across the skin. "Press hard enough to clean the flesh but not so hard that it rips through the hide—or you'll have a moccasin with a hole in it!"

Tongue between his teeth, Daniel hunched over the taut skin and continued to scrape with the flesher until his strokes grew sure and firm. Rachel watched him closely.

"You know, Daniel," she said after he had worked a few minutes in silence, "we shall have to write on the slate from now on. I finished the last of the books today."

"But how will you write what you want to remember?" he asked, looking up from his task with concern.

She wrapped her arms around her bent knees and rested her chin in the slight depression between her legs. "Oh, I've written what's most important," she said. "I saved the last to tell about the Sun Dance. So now I'm finished."

"What's the Sun Dance?" David asked, pausing in his task.

"It's the nation's most important ceremony that takes place when all the tribes come together at the summer solstice."

"Is that when they dance?"

"Yes . . . but it's not really a dance, at least not like the way white men dance. It's to celebrate the warming of the sun, for without its heat the earth wouldn't blossom again each spring, the prairie wouldn't grow rich and plentiful to make the buffalo get fat. It makes the Indians plentiful, too," she said laughing. "Every year many babies are born nine moons after the Sun Dance."

Thoughts of White Hawk flooded her again; it had been after the Sun Dance just a year ago that he first made his feelings known by drawing her within his blanket where they could stand close and speak in private, the first step of Dakota courtship. Remembering made her breath come quicker.

A sudden wind fanned her hair and cooled her neck, damp from where the heavy fall of hair had lain. She lifted it and held it in a pile of tangled curls on top of her head, letting the breeze caress the back of her neck like the soft stroke of a fingertip.

"What else, Rachel?" Daniel asked as he bent his head once more to his task. "What else happens at the dance?"

"Well, it's more than just a dance," she continued, searching for the right words. It was important that Daniel understand the Sun Dance and why it was the center of the tribe's existence. "If a young man wants to be a truly worthy brave," she said, choosing the words carefully, "he must do the Sun Dance to seek the vision that will let him find the true way of life. But to prove he is worthy of such a gift, he must first endure great pain. If you were a Dakota boy . . ." She paused, aware of the concentration on his face, still so childlike, as he plied the flesher. She tried to imagine him as an Indian boy.

Daniel glanced up at her with a dubious expression. "What would I have to do?"

"Well, first—on the morning of the ceremony—you would go to the sweat tipi to be purified."

"What's a—a sweat tipi?"

"It's a special tipi built with a deep hole in the center where heated stones are placed. When you entered, the older braves would give you a bucket of water; and after you had taken off your clothes and closed the flap so no steam could escape, you would throw the water on the hot stones. The stream would make you sweat, and that way you would be cleansed and made pure."

"Whew! It makes me sweat just thinking about it!" he said and wiped his perspiring forehead with his arm. "Then what?"

"Well, while you're in the sweat tipi, the other braves cut a tall straight tree and place it upright in the center of the circle where the dance is to be. They place four colored flags around the tree—yellow to the east where the sun rises, red to the south for the heat of the noonday sun, black to the west for the storm clouds that bring rain, and white to the north for the winter snows.

"Then you would come out of the sweat tipi and lie down near the tree. The *Wicasa-Wakan* would come and—"

"What's that?" Daniel interrupted.

"That's a he," she said, laughing at the perplexed look on his face. "He's like our father and the doctor together. He's the most holy man in the tribe. He would come and cut a small slit through the skin of your chest with a knife."

Daniel's mouth dropped open. "What for?" he asked, staring at her in consternation.

"That's what the dance is all about. The *Wicasa-Wakan* would take a leather rope with a hook on the end. He'd tie one end to the tree. The other end he would hook into the slit in your chest. Then you would stand up and slowly back away from the tree until the rope was taut. You would dance facing the sun while everyone in the tribe watched in a circle around you."

The flesher lay forgotten beside him. "All by myself?" he asked.

"No, probably not. Usually the Sun Dance is performed with four braves." With the hammer she pulled the nails from the ground and lifted the cleaned skin onto the plank. "Now it's ready for tanning. Then we'll smoke it over the fire to keep the rain and water out."

She took the bowl with the rabbit's brain and liver and added some of the fat scraped from the skin. With her fingers she kneaded the substance until it was the consistency of thick, gray cream.

"Ugh!" Daniel said, wrinkling up his face as he looked in the bowl. "You do this part, Rachel."

Dipping her fingers into the mixture, Rachel worked it into the scraped side of the skin, kneading it, squeezing it against the board. "See," she said, "it's just like making bread."

Daniel watched her closely as she took another dab of the mixture and repeated the process. "How long do you have to do that?"

"Until the skin is very soft. A deerskin takes many days. We would have to soak it and then let it dry with a mixture of ashes and water to strip the hair. A rabbit skin won't take so long. We can finish it this afternoon.

Don't you want to try?" She moved aside to make room for him at the board.

Gingerly, his nose wrinkled to avoid the odor, he took some of the mixture in his hands and repeated what she had done.

"That's it," she said after a moment, "that's the way to do it. You'd make a fine Indian, Daniel!"

"What else would I do at the dance, Rachel?" he asked as he kneaded the skin with his small fingers.

"Well, while the four of you are dancing, the drums begin to beat." She closed her eyes. She could see the dance taking place before her as clearly as though she were there. "Together you move slowly around and face each direction until you complete the circle and return to face the sun. Then, as the sun moves higher and the day grows hotter, you begin again, dancing in the circle, pulling against the hook fastened in your chest. Finally the hook tears lose from your flesh and you're free."

Daniel's hands fell still as he stared at Rachel without blinking.

"Why do they want to hurt themselves like that?" he asked in a whisper.

Rachel looked into his solemn eyes. How could she ever make him understand, this white-skinned boy who had never seen the beauty of the dance or the splendor of the tribes? He had never witnessed the power of the vision these young men sought. Often White Hawk had spoken of these visions and explained how enduring the pain and moving through it allowed a man to discover the purpose of his life.

Rachel sighed with regret that Daniel would never

experience such a moment. "It's a great dishonor," she explained, recalling White Hawk's words as he spoke of the ceremony, "not to withstand the pain and tear the flesh free of the hook. And all the while you are dancing with this burning pain and pulling your flesh against the hook, the sun is beating down on you and you are given no food or water. But gradually the feeling of pain dims until your mind is free of thought or feeling. Then it is open to the vision, ready to see the path your life must follow. It is like a journey to a distant and wondrous place where no one has ever walked before."

So powerful was the image that her hand reached to grasp the skin of her chest where the hook would be lodged. Her hand pressed tight against her breast, holding the image within. Slowly her eyes turned back to Daniel and she saw his eyes fixed on her hand, staring in fear and wonder. Gently she took his hand within her own and held it beneath her breast, feeling the quickened beat of her heart.

"To be successful, Daniel . . ." she said, and her voice deepened, vibrant with the wonder she hoped he could feel as well. ". . . to be successful, to see the path and purpose of one's life, is the greatest gift a man can receive for then he need never lose his way."

Daniel bent his head low over the rabbit skin until Rachel couldn't see his face. "I don't think I could be a S-Sioux brave," he said, voice trembling. "I don't think I w-would want to do the Sun Dance."

"That's because you're still a boy. But I know, when the right time came, you'd be very brave. You would win great respect, I know it." He looked so forlorn she reached out an arm to hug him.

"Rachel! Daniel!" Without warning, their father's voice stung them from behind.

Together, Rachel and Daniel swung around to face him, too stunned to reply.

18

So absorbed had Rachel and Daniel been that neither heard their father approach. They looked up at him from the ground; in his black suit he seemed to stretch above them like a dark shadow hovering over the bright afternoon. Rachel wondered how long he had been behind them, watching, listening.

He pointed to the rabbit skin with a rigid finger while ice-blue eyes appraised the bowl and flesher.

His voice cut with a sharp edge. "Daniel! What are you doing?"

Caught unawares, Daniel clamped his lips closed and thrust his hands deep into the pockets of his homespun overall.

Rachel tried to intercede. "He killed a rabbit, Father. With the slingshot Peter gave him."

"Rachel! Be quiet!" He turned to confront her, his face pinched with the anger he struggled to contain. "I'm speaking to Daniel, not you! You've done enough damage! Keep still for once!"

Speechless, Rachel could only stand and stare at him. Never had she been rebuked so sharply, but this time she had earned his wrath. How unforgivable to lose track of the time!—how stupid not to know he might arrive home earlier than usual. She had been too engrossed in her own concerns and now Daniel would be the one who had to answer for her thoughtlessness. A broken promise would have been so much easier to mend!

Her father turned again to Daniel. "I can see it was a rabbit, Daniel," he continued in an icy tone, his finger still pointing at the forbidden objects, "but it's very clear you're not just skinning it. Now tell me—and I want the truth, I'll tolerate no lies!—tell me exactly what you're doing here." He moved his finger a fraction of an inch to Rachel's flesher. "What is that object?"

"Th-that's Rachel's flesher, Father."

"And what, may I inquire, were you doing with it?"

Daniel's soft voice was almost a whisper. "W-we were t-t-tanning the rabbit skin."

"And what were you going to do with this skin?"

"N-nothing, Father. Just k-keep it."

Rachel's anger erupted. No one had the right to humiliate another human being this way, especially a child! But to speak out would only enrage him more. Catching her lower lip between her teeth, she pressed her palms against her thighs to keep herself from springing at him.

"And have you tanned skins like this before, Daniel?" Rachel heard the reasonable tone of the question but she sensed a trap.

"No, Father! Never!" Daniel exclaimed.

Rachel wanted to cry out, warn him to be careful, but the cry was lost somewhere inside her. She could only watch as her father sprang his trap.

"Then you couldn't possibly know how to do it, could you?—unless someone showed you!" The voice lashed out. "Who showed you, Daniel?" Daniel stared at him, unmoving, unable to turn his eyes away. "It was Rachel, wasn't it? Rachel is teaching you her Indian ways, isn't she?" The words caught Daniel full force, but he never blinked or moved. "Isn't she?"

"Yes," he whispered at last.

"You know what the punishment is for disobedience, don't you Daniel?" The finger turned to point at Daniel, and Rachel barely heard his tremulous reply.

"Y-yes, Father."

Their father unfastened his belt and pulled it from the trouser loops until it hung in a straight line before him. "Bend over."

Slowly Daniel obeyed. He bent at the waist, locking his arms behind his knees to steady himself.

"Father, don't!" Rachel cried. "It's not his fault! I was the one!"

His eyes flickered to her face. "I'll deal with you later. Disobedience is a sin I will not tolerate from any of my children." He raised his arm over Daniel's stooped body.

In one swift motion the arm fell, the leather cracking as it landed on Daniel's hunched back. Daniel's face contorted, his eyes squeezed together, but he didn't cry out.

"Father! Please don't!" Rachel cried. "Please don't hit him again!" But the belt cracked a second time. Tears leaked from under Daniel's closed lids, but he held his lips tightly shut.

Rachel wanted to throw herself at her father, hit him

until *he* cried out in pain! She wanted to sink her teeth into the hand holding the belt until that hand bled.

The belt fell a third time and Daniel dropped to his knees.

"No!" In a frenzy Rachel lunged toward her father and grasped his arm. With all her strength she held it to keep it from rising again. She stiffened, expecting the force of her father's strength to cast her aside, but he only stood looking down at Daniel kneeling on the ground. The belt hung limp by her father's side.

"Never mind," he said, his voice suddenly calm, "It's finished. Three is all. Three is enough."

In amazement Rachel let go of her father's arm. "How can you do that?" she asked. "How can you beat a child?" Never in seven years with the Dakota had she seen a child struck.

"How else can a child learn?" he snapped back at her. "Daniel knows well enough he gets three lashes with the belt for disobeying, don't you, Daniel?"

From the ground Daniel looked up at his father and dumbly nodded.

"I will not tolerate disobedience," their father repeated.

Rachel wanted to kneel beside Daniel, to hold him close, but something in his face held her where she stood. The tears had already dried on his cheeks. He had not cried out. He was fighting his own battle in a place where there was no room for a sister's comforting arms.

"Go to your room until suppertime, Daniel," her father ordered. "Pray for forgiveness. Reflect on your folly. I expect this never to happen again!"

Without reply Daniel slowly got to his feet and

trudged toward the house. Rachel waited, seething, until the door had closed behind him.

"Are you going to beat *me* now, Father?" She spat the words. "I am your child and I have disobeyed you!"

Her father stared at her without speaking, and Rachel could not fathom what lay locked in his heart or in the depths of those hooded eyes.

"No matter what monstrous things you may wish to believe of me," he said at last in a tired voice, "I am not a woman-beater. I have asked little of you, Rachel," he continued with a sigh, "except that you give up your Indian ways and become a God-fearing woman once again. Is that so very much to ask?" With the toe of his boot he nudged the flesher lying in the grass. "I shudder to think what your mother must be feeling as she looks down upon you. Indians caused her death. At least have the decency not to flaunt their ways in this household!"

His eyes held Rachel. Numb, drained of energy, she could not look away. "I haven't the heart for this," he said in a low voice. "I shall pray for your salvation." With slow step and hunched shoulders he climbed the stoop and disappeared into the house.

Rachel stood alone in the yard, left with only a deep, aching sorrow. The unhappiness she had caused both Daniel and her father pressed harder. She had inflicted enough pain.

She must get away from this house, the town, ride out on the prairie far from the trials of the white man's world. If only Peter had not left she could have begged him for the use of his horse.

In the shed the old cart horse Nugget nickered, reminding Rachel of his presence. He might not carry her like the wind, but he could at least carry her faster than her own legs.

She led him from the shed, grasped his mane with both hands and swung across his back. Startled at the unfamiliar weight, Nugget arched his neck and side-stepped; but Rachel held him steady and he responded to her reassuring murmur and the firm pressure of her knees.

Rachel urged him into a canter as she rode from the yard, down the pathway to the road from town where she turned northward. Once clear of the house, she slowed the lumbering horse to a trot. She had not been astride a horse since the day Aunt Sarah had arrived. How good to have the solid flesh beneath her again, to savor the feel of Nugget's sturdy back between her legs, the wind against her face.

A mile beyond the house the road narrowed into a rough wagon trail. She slowed Nugget to a walk and let him follow the ruts for another few miles before turning west across the open prairie toward the river. The afternoon sun was still hot. A light haze of dust and pollen hung in the warm air.

When she came to one of the narrow streams that flowed into the Missouri River, Rachel pulled the tired horse to a halt and slid from his back in a sparse grove of cottonwoods. She led Nugget to the water for a drink and turned him loose to graze in the tall grass that grew lush and green in the fertile, untilled soil. She unlaced her boots and pulled them off, savoring the feel of the unmown grass under the trees, cool and yielding against the soles of her feet. Kneeling beside the stream, she lowered her face beneath the surface until the water had washed away the dust and the sweat and the last residue of the afternoon's travail.

In the shade of a cottonwood, she sank to the ground and leaned against the firm trunk. She pressed the palms of her hands flat against the earth. Closing her eyes, she let the warm breeze dry her face and listened to a distant meadowlark sing as the wind in the leaves above echoed the bird's hymn.

How she had missed this simple act of sitting on the ground, of being at one with the earth! She pressed her palms hard against the firm soil and felt the faint pulse within her wrist beat to the rhythm of earth and sky. Earth's voice is heard through the heart and she had closed her heart to its song. Her father had taught her to set apart one day as holy; how quickly she had forgotten that all days are sacred and the gift of the Creator. Here was her altar, her sanctuary against pain and grief, her place of worship.

She had been away too long, and away from nature a man's heart grows hard. The old ones knew that, the elders of the tribe who kept the young ones close to earth's softening breast. She had allowed earth's voice to fade, listened too long to the human voice that clamored like a false prophet.

A strange sickness preyed on her soul, an ailment as unfathomable and deadly as the disease that killed Aunt Sarah. How long would it be before some other sickness beset her, destroying her body as well as her soul? At Aunt Sarah's funeral two women had spoken of such things, unaware of her presence behind them. *Such a pity*, one had said to the other. *But Sarah Jessup isn't the only one. I've heard tell the same has happened to others come back from living with the Indians, this sickness and early death. So peculiar*, the other had answered, *don't they know the cause? No*, the first had replied, *they just up and die.*

Up and die. Rachel could hear the voice as clearly now as on the day the words were spoken. She thought of the fever that had struck her last winter and the strange lassitude and fatigue she had been feeling lately. What would be next? Those women at Aunt Sarah's funeral had given her warning. She must heed that warning. Somehow she must find a way to go home again, home to the tribe and her life on the open prairie.

She must let the voices of earth and sky speak the wisdom of Wakan-Tanka. If she listened, the path would open before her. She had seen through the glass darkly. Now, if she opened her heart, she would see face to face; the way would become clear.

She opened her eyes and gazed up through the shadowy branches, freed at last from the weight of her longing and guilt.

She started back to the house as the sun began to set and rode into the yard just as darkness fell, prepared to bear the full brunt of her father's wrath; but only Nina was standing on the back stoop and came with a lantern to meet her.

"You've caused me a lot of worry and more than a few gray hairs!" Nina said with asperity and grasped Nugget's mane as Rachel slid from his back.

In the lantern's light Nina's face looked drawn and

tired, and Rachel was suddenly aware of her own bone-aching weariness. She had been the cause of seemingly endless anguish today—to herself, to her father, to Daniel, and now even to Nina who had always treated her with kindness. She wanted to put her arms around Nina's neck, to hold her and beg her forgiveness for all the pain she had caused, but she was too exhausted to do more than whisper, "I'm sorry, Nina. I won't be so late again."

"Never mind. You're home safe now. Your supper's setting on the hearth. Go and eat. I'll stable Nugget."

Grateful, Rachel turned toward the house and then paused. "Where's Father?" she asked.

"Old Mrs. Stowell died this afternoon. He's gone to be with the family—and had to depend on them for a ride, I might add."

One more in her litany of thoughtless acts that day. "I'm sorry," Rachel repeated, "I never thought . . . " She opened the door.

"Daniel's in bed, Rachel. He told me what happened this afternoon. He wants to see you before he goes to sleep." Nina pulled Nugget's mane and headed him toward the shed, then stopped. "You mustn't judge your father harshly." With her back to Rachel, Nina's voice was muffled. "He only gets angry because he knows you are unhappy and because he loves you—loves all of his children—so much. You know that, don't you?"

"Yes," Rachel said softly, "I do know that."

"Good." Nina disappeared into the shadow of the shed.

Inside, Rachel tiptoed to the door of Daniel's small room.

"Daniel, are you still awake?" she called in a hushed voice, fearing to wake him if he slept.

"Is that you, Rachel?" Daniel's sleepy voice replied. "I was afraid you'd gone away."

She knelt beside his small trundle bed and felt his warm breath on her cheek. "I'm sorry I caused you trouble this afternoon," she said softly, brushing back a lock of damp hair from his forehead.

"I didn't mind, Rachel. Really." He raised up on one elbow and in the light from the doorway his dark eyes shone. "I was a worthy brave, wasn't I?" His small voice held only the shadow of a doubt. "Wasn't I, Rachel?"

"Oh yes, Daniel," she said and hugged him close, her voice a whisper to mask the tears that rose in her throat. "*Toketu ceyas.* No one could ever be a more worthy brave."

She held him close until his breathing grew quiet. His arms fell limp at his sides and his eyes closed in sleep, a young bird with untried wings, not yet able to fly from the nest. But what he had proved to himself that afternoon would never desert him.

Careful not to disturb the boy, Rachel rose to her feet. For all of her firm determination to go home again, somehow to make the journey back to the tribe and her Dakota family, when she looked down at Daniel asleep, that determination faltered.

Rachel knew then that the hardest thing she might ever have to do would be to set off on her journey alone, to walk away and leave her brother Daniel behind.

19

T he dream of journeying north beckoned Rachel without respite. At each turning in the road, each bend of the river, the whispered call became a song, a chant, pulling her northward to *Paha Sapa*, summoning her home.

She heard it on misty nights when fog curled inland from the river and on windy days when rain swept from the hills to wash the grass grown gray with dust. She heard it at dusk in the hoofbeats of deer in flight and at daybreak in the owl's last cry. Then Rachel would hold her breath and turn northward, hearing the spirit's voice calling her home.

The fatigue, the ache in her bones had become more constant now. She must hurry. If she waited much longer . . . .

But how? The question endlessly churned in her mind, but every answer presented another obstacle. The distance was too far to walk; vast wilderness stretched between St. Joseph and Fort Tecumseh at the northern end of the river. Too many dangers lurked there—hunger, exposure, wild animals, not to mention renegade Indians and white hunters. A solitary white girl would be lucky ever to survive the journey on foot.

With a horse she might risk the journey alone; but although Nugget could manage a few miles, he would never last that great a distance nor the rigor of an unbroken trail. To steal a horse was unthinkable; it would only invite pursuit.

There was only one other way—to return home the way she had come, on the steamboat *Yellowstone*. But she needed money for passage, and she would have no way of earning any without revealing why she needed it.

Always she returned to the only possible solution. At first, it seemed too unlikely for conjecture; but as one week passed into another, she knew it was her only hope. She must ask her father to send her home and pay her way north as he had paid to bring her south.

He had been strangely silent since their confrontation over Daniel's rabbit, taciturn even with Nina. And Rachel had often looked up to find his eyes following her, assessing, measuring, coldly judging under those hooded lids.

Each time she thought of facing him, her heart sank. Such a request could only enrage him, bolster his determination to keep her in St. Joseph against her will.

But there was no other way.

*

On a clear morning late in June, Rachel awoke before daybreak and breathed a deep sigh. Today she must ask Father to let her go. But what if, for all her pleading, he refused? What then?

She shivered, pushing away the thought, but her stomach churned as she entered the kitchen and found her father already at the table. Her hands trembled as she set his daily bowl of porridge in front of him. No one seemed to notice.

"Rachel, eat your breakfast," Nina admonished as Rachel toyed with her bowl of steaming oatmeal. "You're growing thin as a rail!"

Her father frowned at her over his spoon. "Have to keep up your strength. Mustn't have you getting sick," he said around a mouthful of oatmeal and returned his attention to his own bowl. When it was empty, he carefully rolled up his napkin and pushed it firmly through the wooden napkin ring, always his final act before rising from a meal.

Rachel gripped the seat of her chair with both hands.

"Father, I must talk with you!" The words tumbled out in a rush.

Rising, he paused to look at her, but she didn't continue. "Yes?" he questioned after a moment.

She couldn't ask him now, not here in front of both Nina and Daniel.

"At the church," she blurted. "Perhaps I could come to the church?"

"I have an appointment," he said, "and then I must make a visitation." He lifted the gold watch from his pocket and looked at it. "Why don't you come in—say, about an hour? I should be free by then."

"An hour," she repeated in assent. "Thank you, Father." Her voice was like a thin wind, and she felt certain her face revealed her agitation; but her father made no further comment except to tell Nina he might be a little late for dinner.

After he left, Rachel escaped Nina's questioning eyes

by fleeing to the chicken coop to gather the eggs. If only she could confide in Nina, pour out her fears and longings. But if Nina tried to persuade her not to leave, she knew she would lose heart. She could not risk weakening in her resolve now.

By the time she returned to the house with the eggs, Nina and Daniel were nowhere in sight. Rachel slipped quietly from the house. Nina would know where she had gone.

During the walk to town, Rachel took little notice of where she was going. She tried to rehearse what she would say to convince her father, the words she would use to plead with him, but her mind was in such a turmoil that the words became a meaningless jumble.

The church was quiet. The windows were open and a cool breeze stirred the gauze curtains, pulled closed to keep out the flies. She paused for a moment at the entrance, aware for the first time of how peaceful the church was with no one there, how restful with its plain whitewashed walls and wooden benches.

On tiptoe she walked down the center aisle. As she passed the altar she stopped to look up at the figure of Jesus hanging on the cross.

How sad he looked gazing down at her, his arms outstretched, his thin legs twisted in the agony of being nailed to the cross. How close he seemed! Surely he would understand what she was feeling and tell her to go back, return to the tribe, to Waoka and Ina, Tanka and White Hawk. This mournful Jesus would say, If you have looked deep into your heart, then you must follow what it knows to be true.

The churning calmed, the jumbled thoughts stilled. She made her way to the back of the church where Sunday school was held and where her father had his office. She knocked on the door and entered.

The room was dim, lit only by one small window facing north. The furnishings were simple: some wooden shelves lined with a matching set of books bound in red tooled leather, an old roll-top desk with an unadorned ladderback chair beside it. Her father sat behind the desk in his swivel chair, his back to her. Through the window Rachel could see the small graveyard behind the church and the two neighboring graves: her mother, buried now almost eight years, and Aunt Sarah whose grave was newly turned. Was her father thinking of them also?

"Father?" Her voice sounded hollow in the small room. He did not respond. She drew a deep breath and continued.

"Father, I must ask you—beg of you—" Her voice broke and she drew a deep breath. She must not falter now. "Father, I want you to let me go back."

"I suspected that was why you were coming, Rachel," he said without turning around, his voice expressionless. She wanted to see his face, to read what he was feeling, discover how hard the fight would be. "I thought that's what you were going to ask, and I have been considering what I would say to you," he continued in the same even tone after a moment's silence. "I have tried to think what your mother would have me do, what words I could say that might change your mind."

He swung the chair around to face her. His eyes were as deeply shadowed as the slopes of *Paha Sapa* at nightfall. She couldn't bring herself to ask for his answer, not yet.

"How . . . how did you know, Father—that I would ask?" The words were no more than a whisper.

"Nina knew."

Rachel looked at him in surprise. "How could Nina have known?"

"She's known all along—almost from the beginning. She tried to warn me often enough, but of course I wouldn't listen . . . didn't want to listen. Then, after Sarah died, she said it would be soon." His long slender fingers lay knitted in his lap as though she had interrupted him at prayer. He pressed his forefingers against the high bridge of his nose and closed his eyes. "What can I say that won't make you hate me?"

In his question she had her answer. He was not going to let her leave. But she had not expected otherwise. She exhaled slowly.

"I can't hate you, Father, although at one time I thought I could." She struggled to keep her voice steady and to hide the deep disappointment. She pressed her arms tightly against her sides. "I don't ask to go back because I want to leave you, Father, but only because I don't belong here. My life is out there," she said, gesturing toward the window, "under the sky, on the open plains—not in a town like St. Joseph. I can't be happy here, Father."

"I have reconciled myself to that fact, Rachel," he said, following her gesture with his eyes as he folded his hands once more in his lap. "A father harbors the hope that his child can find happiness in this life, and I hoped such would be true for you. But my greater love must be for your immortal soul. No, Rachel," he said and shook his head, giving emphasis to the denial. "I'm sorry, but for the sake of your soul I cannot send you back to that heathen culture."

"But my immortal soul means nothing to me!" Rachel stared at him, astounded. "Why can't you care about what happens to me *now*, and let me go back to my family?"

"*We* are your family." His eyes flashed with familiar sparks although his voice remained quiet.

Rachel struggled to find the words that might make him relent. "You have no right to deal with what you can't understand!" She lashed out at him recklessly, no longer caring what she said. "You can't know. For you it's simple, but I'm not like you. I am not one person but two. I live in two worlds, speak two languages, belong to two families, know two claims upon my heart. How can you know what it's like to be torn between two parts of your own self?" Tears ran down her face and she brushed at them impatiently, intent only on making him understand. "How can you know what it's like to have two shadows always at war within you?"

The silence in the small office was so complete that she could hear the whisper of a bird's wing as it brushed the leaves on the lilac beside the window.

"I do know what it's like, Rachel," her father said at last, and his voice was heavy and deep. "I do know, and I should have known you carried this heavy burden as well. I have been very remiss indeed. All these months I have given so little thought to . . . to what you must be feeling . . . "

His words trailed off and he half turned in his chair to face the window as though he heard another voice somewhere beyond it. "If you only knew what doubts I harbored in all those long years of searching for you! Can you understand—I think perhaps you can—that I was as afraid of finding you as I was of not ever seeing you again?" His hands hung between his knees. "And the longer we searched, the more I questioned if I could love the stranger you had become, a daughter without creed, perhaps without language, without the bedrock of affection born of shared family time and a shared faith."

He blinked against the light and drew a deep, shuddering breath. "You speak of warring shadows! And all those years I was a man of peace bursting with anger, a man who preached the healing power of love who was enraged by the fate of two of my children."

The room spun. Rachel grasped the edge of the desk for support. How little she knew him. How much easier it had been not to know him, to hold him at a distance that placed guards upon the heart. Never had she guessed the doubts that plagued him, the torment his spirit had battled daily.

"But how could you endure, Father?" she whispered. "How could you survive such agony?"

"There was only one way," he replied slowly. "I could survive only by choosing one side of myself and denying the other forever. But now I am obliged to war against that other side for the rest of my life. Sometimes, Rachel, life brings difficult choices indeed, and we must learn to accept the will of God."

"That's all very well for you, Father," Rachel cried, and dropped to her knees beside him, imploring him with her eyes as well as her words. "But if I have to pretend that these past seven years never existed, then what will be left for me?" She clutched at the one argument she was certain he could not counter. "If I stay here, Father, I know I will die."

A spark of fear flared in his eyes. "Nina said the same thing," he said, almost in a whisper. "Why are you so sure?"

"At Aunt Sarah's funeral, I heard a woman speak of others who came back only to die—and I know it's true."

"Surely you don't believe such gossip!"

"But it happened to Aunt Sarah, Father, and I know it will happen to me! I *must* go back."

"I had so hoped . . . prayed . . . that in time you'd forget them and want only us. Now I can see it's not to be." He looked into her upturned face, and Rachel saw her own unhappiness reflected in her father's eyes. "I see I must lose you after all." He half turned in his chair and faced the window again. "How much must a man be expected to give up?" His words were directed somewhere beyond the room.

Was there a spirit voice he heard as well? Rachel waited in silence, hardly daring to breathe.

"I've lost a wife, a son, and now"—his lips trembled as he blinked his eyes against the tears that filled them—"now must I lose my daughter as well?"

"No, Father, not lose! Never lose! Not if you allow me to go back!" Her arms circled his legs as she exhaled a great rush of breath. He was going to let her leave after all! "I'll always be your daughter, Father," she said and leaned her forehead against his knee. "And if you'll have me, I would like to come back to visit . . . when I can."

"Whenever you wish—" He lifted her chin and brushed his lips against the crown of her hair. "And knowing that will help me bear your leaving." She looked up and saw tears rimming the eyes that were a mirrored image of her own. Cupping her chin in the palm of his hand, he bent his head and his lips moved lightly against hers. Their touch was pleasant and cool.

With a sigh he leaned back in his chair. "I hope you will be able to come soon," he said. "Your leaving will be very hard on Daniel."

At the reminder of the task that still awaited her, a knot of dread settled in her stomach. "I know," she said, "and I only hope I have the courage to tell him."

"I imagine Nina will help prepare the way. It will go easier if he knows you will be back."

"I have much to thank Nina for."

"Nina's a remarkable woman." He shook his head in wonder. "Perhaps, in part, that's why I . . . why I have sometimes let anger rule me," he continued almost to himself. "I hated to think she might be right. But I should have known better."

"And I, Father," Rachel said quietly. "I know how long you searched to find me, and how hard it must be to give me up again. Thank you for letting me go."

"There's one thing I must ask," he said in a low voice, and the light filtering in the window deepened the lines ridging his fair skin. "One thing you must promise me." His eyes shone with the intensity of what he was feeling.

Rachel waited, dreading what he was going to say.

"When you return . . . no matter how often . . . you must never speak of . . . of them or of your life with them."

"I promise, Father," Rachel said in a whisper.

A flicker of doubt crossed his face. "I just don't think I could stand to hear about . . . any of it," he said and covered his eyes with his hand.

"I promise, Father," she said again and placed her palm on the back of his hand that shielded his eyes from her.

The knowledge that Kata Wi and Rachel must always remain apart filled her with sadness. Never would she be able to make the two lives come together. Here she would always have to pretend what was most important in her life didn't exist.

But compared to what her father was giving up, it was a small sacrifice, and perhaps some day he would soften. Perhaps in time he might accept the whole of her, not just a small part. In the meantime, she would keep her promise.

During the walk home, both were silent, each lost in thought. As they neared the house, Rachel could see Daniel waiting for them, swinging on the gate at the end of the long drive. Dread settled once more in the pit of her stomach.

"You must promise me something else, Rachel," her father said, breaking the silence. "You won't say anything that might make Daniel think you aren't coming back. I couldn't bear it for him."

"I know, Father."

She would be careful not to say anything that might cause Daniel unnecessary pain or her father to change his mind about letting her go.

She looked up the road. In the distance Daniel waved to greet them. With a divided heart, Rachel raised her arm to return the salute.

20

Rachel stood on the dock and watched the pale sun inch its way upward behind the mist. She remembered the last time she had stood here with her father—and the look on his face when he had first seen her.

That seemed a lifetime ago.

She looked down at her shoes, black and shiny from the polishing Nina had lovingly given them the night before, and remembered how long it had taken her to get used to them. The flowered dimity dress she wore, her best dress, was clean and starched, and rustled when she moved. Across her shoulders hung a light shawl, one that Leah had knitted for her before the wedding.

How peculiar she would look to the tribe and her Dakota family. Perhaps they wouldn't recognize this strange white girl in the ruffled cotton skirt. But when they looked beyond the clothes, they would know her—she was sure of it.

Her father paced nervously while the dockhands worked to get the gangplank in place. Only two other passengers waited with them, a young man and his bride who didn't seem to notice anyone else.

"Do you have everything you need?" her father asked

for the third time, and she smiled and nodded. "The money's in a safe place?"

"Yes, Father." She patted her waist.

"And the letter to the agent? You make sure he hires out a decent horse. Heaven only knows how far you'll have to ride from Fort Tecumseh."

"Yes, Father, I will. But it won't be far." Her heart beat faster in anticipation. Just a few more days . . .

Early this morning she and her father had left the house quietly in order not to awaken Daniel. Last night she had said a final good-bye to him, the hardest task she had ever performed. His round face had crumpled as his eyes filled with tears.

"Don't cry, Daniel," Rachel whispered, blinking back her own tears as she remembered her first morning in St. Joseph when she had knelt in the kitchen with Daniel's arms around her and he had said those same words to comfort her. For Daniel's sake she would not give way now. "I don't want to leave you," she said quietly, "but I must. Just for a little while."

"You promise you'll come back soon?"

She nodded and hugged him close. "Soon—I promise, and until then, I have something to give you," she said.

"A present?" Daniel blinked hard and the tears retreated as he looked at her expectantly. "What is it, Rachel?"

She reached into the large pocket in her apron and drew out the exercise books Peter had given her, filled now to the last page.

"Oh, Rachel, your *book*?" Daniel's face was full of wonder.

"I want you to have it, Daniel. But you must keep it in a safe place and read it only when you're alone," she cautioned. "No one must know that you have it."

"But don't you want it, Rachel?"

"Now that I'm going back, I won't need it . . . for a while. And as long as you have it, I'll know you won't forget me." Bending above the pillow, she kissed him on the cheek. How soft and warm it was.

"Don't go, Rachel! Stay with me!"

"I'll stay till you're fast asleep," she promised. "Scoot down now and I'll tuck you in." He snuggled under the covers and she knelt by the bed to tuck the sheet around him. "Now close your eyes."

"I'll miss you Rachel." His eyes closed tightly against threatening tears.

"I'll miss you, too," she whispered, "but just keep remembering—I'll be back someday soon."

"Rachel?"

"I'm still here."

His voice grew sleepy. "Your book—that's the best present I could ever have." Sighing, he drifted into sleep. Rachel kissed him softly on the lips and tiptoed from the room.

When she came out, Nina was waiting with the knapsack of food.

"For your trip," she said. "It's a long journey. You'll be needing it." She turned away and blew her nose but after a moment spoke again. "If you don't come back . . . if for some reason I might not see you again. . . . " She shook her head and wiped her eyes, unable to continue.

Rachel reached her arms around her. "I'll miss you, Nina!" she said. "And thank you—not just for the food but for everything. I don't know what I would have done without you!" She held Nina tight and smelled the familiar odors of lye soap and yeast. "You know, there's one thing that Father and I do agree on."

Nina smiled. "What's that?"

"Father says you're a remarkable woman."

"He said that?"

For the first time in Rachel's recollection, Nina had blushed.

*

On the dock, as Rachel watched the sun move above the horizon, the gangplank banged into place and the dock-workers carried on the bales of cargo to be shipped upriver. The *Yellowstone* was ready for boarding. Oblivious to their surroundings, the man and wife walked on board arm in arm. The wheel began to churn and overhead a ship's whistle blew three raucous blasts. The *Yellowstone* was ready to move out.

Rachel picked up the knapsack of food. She turned to her father who stood with his back to her.

"Good-bye, Father," she said softly, laying her hand on his arm. She reached around to kiss him and saw tears rolling down his cheeks.

His arms went around her and she hugged him to her; then she turned to the gangplank, no longer able to hold back her own tears.

From behind her she heard his voice call out.

"Come back soon, Rachel!"

Forcing a smile, she turned to wave.

The gangplank was pulled aboard and the *Yellowstone* moved slowly away from the dock.

Alone, Rachel stood at the stern rail and looked over the churning wheel, straining to see the diminishing figure in the black serge suit standing on the dock. As the boat swung around the first bend in the river, her father was lost from sight.

The rawness of early morning on the river seeped into her bones and she felt a chill. The sun, a pale, white-gold ball, lifted above the distant treetops and gradually the mist began to burn away.

Rachel turned from the stern and made her way forward to the bow that cut a path in the water leading north. She lifted her face to the wind, looking far up the river whose farthest bank marked the beginning of the great grazing plains to the west.

Somewhere ahead, White Hawk would be riding through the grass, leaning into the wind.

Somewhere ahead, not far from the sacred hills of the crystal cave, the hills of *Paha Sapa*, the tribe would be camped. Perhaps they still watched for the girl Kata Wi; perhaps even now they were waiting for her.

Overhead, the sun burned through the last veil of mist, a circle of fire rising on its journey from earth to sky.